THE DEVIL'S THROAT

LYNN HAYWOOD

D0552899

Printed by Amazon

The Devil's Throat

Lynn Haywood has asserted her right under the Copyright, Designs and Patents Act 1988 to be identified as the author of this work.

©2019 Lynn Haywood

ISBN: 978-1796953770

Cover Design by Tree

I would like to thank my husband, Colin, and my children Andrew and Emily for their support and faith in me re-writing and editing this novel after 25 years tucked away in a file.

Even before the 19th century seamen referred to Cromer Bay as 'The Devil's Throat'. A place where gale force winds drove vessels to the rocks and flat shores of Cromer.

Chapter One

Cromer, North Norfolk, England
December, 1870

Charlotte drew back the curtains, below her, shadowy silhouettes of the townsfolk were running down the alley in pelting rain, they held their lanterns high swaying light back and forth. She ran from her bedroom and dashed down the narrow winding staircase.

She was surprised to find her mother sitting in a fireside chair in the parlour; her mother was similarly dressed as her, a black woollen skirt and a threadbare gansey over a white blouse. The fire crackled, the clock on the mantelpiece ticked one second, two seconds, the bells struck again. Candle-flames either side of the clock wavered. Charlotte could smell tobacco. Henry had been here while she had been sleeping. He had left his dog-headed pipe upside down in an ashtray on a small round table beside the other fireside chair. Outside the wind howled and whistled through gaps in the small window panes. Her mother lifted up her knitting; click, click went her needles. Charlotte could see the rib of the collar, the cuffs at the end of long sleeves, cuffs double stitched and folded.

Sally ignored her daughter and admired her latest knitted stretch of stocking stitch and the intricate herring bones twisted in the ropes knotted coils. She wanted to check the sails of John's boat but she couldn't find them. She wanted to tread in the deep etched narrow lanes of the sea-bed where John held the reins of sea-horses. They were galloping over the white-washed bed of starfish writhing their fat pulp bodies, meandering their thousands of suckers. She couldn't map his route home through the deep ridges at the bottom of the sea.

She laughed out loud seeing her pink slippers on her feet, a new gansey on her knee.

'Mother!' Charlotte shook her mother. 'Mother the church bells! Are you coming? Are you well enough to carry a lantern?'

Charlotte stared into her mother's ashen face, blonde wisps of hair escaped from her loosely tied bun. There was no time for discussion with her mother, she'd have to leave her behind, and anyway the gale-force wind would most likely lift her right off her feet.

Charlotte padded over the floorboards into the kitchen.

A fire was burning here too. She cursed Henry for lighting the parlour fire. They had little enough fuel for one room never mind two, though with hindsight he may have stocked up the coal-house with logs or more coal. The black kettle was cold on the hearth; two unwashed white sheets were slung over the clothes horse. Henry must have ousted Will from his bed into their mother's bed in case there was a chance of a lodger for a few nights.

My, Henry was quick, and how comfortable he has made himself in our house, she thought, as she walked around the solid oak table and moved a chair to climb up to reach a lantern on the top shelf of the dresser.

'Get me one too,' her mother said in a quiet voice.

'Mother?'

Charlotte knew this was a breakthrough. She'd been weaning her mother off sixpence worth of laudanum per week for the past year, though her mother didn't know it. For the first time since she was ten years old and the six years since her father had gone missing, her mother seemed lucid.

'All right, Mother. But you have to stay close to me.'

Pulling on their boots in the hallway she glanced at the clothes pegs and counted coats.

'Will?' she queried

'Coal-running,' her mother said, looking at the floor guiltily as if she knew Will should not be outside in this treacherous weather.

'He isn't even wearing the old Sou'wester!' exclaimed Charlotte. 'And what about what the doctor said! How could you let him go out in his state?

'Take the oilskin jacket, Mother.'

'No, I—'

'Give me your shawl.'

'But Char—'

'Just do it, Mother.'

Will shivered, rain ran down the oversized shoddy-stained oilskin coat he wore, it dripped over his shins and gathered in the turned up folds of the sleeves. He tried to shake the rain out at the same time as wiping rivulets of rain which ran down his nose and dripped from his chin. Out at sea 'The Devil's Throat' frothed and foamed white against the pitch blackness, the sea began to lash deep into the undercut of cliff where he was sheltering. Spray showered him, he was sure the sea was trying to swallow him up. He was lithe and quick and ran full pelt away from it to the West Beach while keeping a keen look out for any washed-up spoils from the stricken two-masted schooner.

He could make out a thousand lanterns carried by the townsfolk snaking from the jetty along the stony beach and winding up to the cliff top. The north wind scaled up the cliff whipping through the cocooned yellow flames so they rocked and swayed eerily.

In front of him sand and grit mixed with creamy foam billowed down the dark beach faster than a horse could gallop. He climbed on a three-foot high flint strand line dragging a moth-eaten sack. A rocket launcher shook the ground, it boomed a rope off the beach towards the stranded wreck; the Devil above drowned out the lines whining with a shudder of thunder.

The sinking schooner groaned. For now Will was the only coal-runner on this part of the beach, other beach combers would arrive soon after the rescuers reached the vessel, they'd come down from the cliffs and the town. He glimpsed the schooner by a quarter-moon in a break of cloud. The vessel lurched forwards and backwards, peaks revealing the lifeboat, troughs swallowed the boat back again. The gripping and grinding of muscular arms of the lifeboat men wrestled to reach the survivors in the sand-banked schooner which looked like it might capsize at any given moment.

On the lower shore, Will saw a man struggling in the giant waves, voices called out and he saw two men running. Instinctively Will jumped down from the mound and crouched into the flint stones behind it.

As the man struggled ashore crawling with one arm after other, dragging his legs behind him, the two men went to his aid and pulled him further up the beach.

Something's wasn't right. The two men were leaning over the man; they were going through the man's pockets while he lay fighting them off. The man sat up and lashed out in panic and defence. He was coughing and spluttering and shouted something in a foreign language. The two men struggled to make him lie back down in the shingle.

Will crouched further into the wet stones and peered from behind his hideout and watched one of the men put his hand over the washed-up man's mouth.

He had to go and get help for the man. He stood up and swayed as if all the blood had gone from his head; his leg muscles were frozen and tense too. He was still weak from a cough that had plagued him for a month or two but he'd ventured out driven by the lure of the church bells and the temptation of any wreckage, plus the opportunity to fill his sack with free coal.

One of the men shouted something.

They'd seen him!

Seawater seeped into his thin leather shoes as he splashed through pools towards the steep jetty. From the cliffs a one thousand strong crowd roared, but not for him, the lifeboat must have reached the stricken schooner.

Will ran up the steep cobbled jetty his shoes making a soft splut splut as they pounded on the concreted-in flint stone road. He ran up the paved Jetty Street, past the bathing machine owner's house, past the butcher's, the boot and shoe maker's, the bakery, the beer house; the shop fronts were all in darkness, the cottages between all locked up and empty, everyone had gone to help with lanterns to light the beach for the sinking schooner. He should have run up the cliff to them, not chased after something that turned out to be something he'd rather not have seen.

Now, he turned left at the top of the street and ran into the church yard. He leapt over gargoyles fallen from the broken church roof sure they slathered over slates on the ground.

Will stopped running and paused at a gravestone, he gasped for breaths between coughing fits. Through torrential rain he could see an old spade, piles of flint stones and broken glass amongst barren shrubs and stomped down dead weeds.

He hid behind a leaning gravestone and crouched in muddy soil, hunching his knees to his chest. He could hear and see dark silhouettes of the two men as they began searching systematically for him.

Will recognized the voice of one of the men as they drew closer. Henry?

Would Henry harm him for what he'd seen? Unsure, Will launched himself for the church path which led to an alley and his cottage adjacent to the east side of the church. Henry would never touch him if his mother and Charlotte were home. Charlotte would have gone to the beach but his mother wouldn't have gone would she? She was acting better lately, almost normal on some days ...

Above him the sky cracked with lightning, a dazzling zig-zag tore down from the sky and struck the church roof. Will momentarily curled up into a ball on the ground to protect his head. More roof tiles crumbled down, they were falling on Henry and whoever was with him; they cursed and swore. Will slipped out of the wedged back iron gate into the corner of the alley. He could see his cottage was in darkness. His mother must have gone with Charlotte. On the church side of the alley were several small outbuildings, all he could think to do in the few seconds he had before the men caught up with him was to slip under the door of the laundry-shed. The tall muscular men would never squeeze under the door and hopefully they would think he'd fled down the alley and back to the throng on the clifftop.

He saw a good hiding place in the dolly tub and cramped down inside it.

Chapter Two

Grey December light crept down the alley between the row of cottages and the opposite outbuildings. The light slid under the wooden slats of the ill-fitted door of the laundry shed and alerted Will it was morning as he peeped through the lid of the dolly tub.

'Will?' called Charlotte.

Will heard his sister but he didn't call back. The night had been 'unpredictable'. He repeated the word in his head, maybe he'd use the word in the classroom later to impress his friends. Moisture from being rain-soaked, sea-soaked or the wet-washing clinging to his skin from the over-sized shirt he'd wrapped up in caused him to shiver violently. The tin-dolly had become airless. He decided to abandon his hiding place and he stood up and slung off the round lid, it made a loud clatter on the stone floor.

'Will! Is that you in there?'

He could hear a herring gull cry from the church roof – or thereabouts. He was aware of Charlotte's boots behind the gap under the door.

'Come out, Will.'

The night's storm had passed and petered out like the bells and men's voices.

'I've been going out of my mind with worry. Didn't you hear me searching for you all night?'

Will traced a finger around a waxy sheen on the edge the dolly-tub. He started a coughing fit that wouldn't stop, it hurt his chest and throat.

'Char—get mother, please get mother.'

When they'd returned from the wreckage Charlotte had made her mother go to bed and fabricated some story about Will being in her bed, and then she had ditched the ridiculous black shawl for the oilskin coat and gone out to look for him. But she was still soaked underneath and now she was so cold but at least Will was safe.

Will slept soundly at last. They had made such a commotion on their return to the cottage that the noise had woken their mother, and Sally had shown concern and puzzlement that Charlotte had lied to her about Will. Now, Sally watched over him and adored his blonde eyelashes and the way his curious nose would twitch in his sleep. She smoothed out the sheets and grey blankets and plumped up the patchwork quilt she had made years ago. She used torn strips of an old white sheet to mop his feverish brow. In the pool of the light from the window she pondered on putting coal on the embers of the fire, or should she stoke the embers and let them die out, or should she open the window? Undecided she stroked his blonde hair which badly needed trimming – it fell to his shoulders, and she had begun to notice how he was always tucking his fringe away from his eyes. Sally noted Will's pattern of deepened breathing. He swallowed in his sleep, and she wondered if she should lift him to drink some water. Undecided, she started singing, a cuckoo song he'd loved as a three-year-old. She could only remember the first verse; she quietly sang it to him over and over.

Charlotte was making a broth from chicken bones and the scant vegetables they had left: an old onion; carrots and a swede which was a devil to chop. The broth could stew for hours on the fire in the living room. She was seething that Henry had the nerve to lodge a 'Captain O'Rourke' in Will's bed, which as it happened, didn't matter that much because Will was in his mother's bed. Charlotte hadn't slept all night and even this early the captain was snuggled up asleep while she slaved getting his breakfast. She put the bacon rashers Henry had left for the occasion in the frying pan over the fire, which would sit to the side of spit holding the pan of broth. She could hear her mother humming away at Will's bedside. Charlotte hadn't seen this captain, but apparently Henry had said his two-masted-schooner had come to the aid of the stricken vessel too late to do anything as the lifeboat had got there first.

Charlotte closed her eyes for a second and then quickly moved the frying pan to a colder spot over the fire. She ran upstairs to her room as softly as she could and went to her dressing table. She took stoppers from two scent bottles which had pewter outers so no one could see the contents. What if mother wandered into her room and looked in the scent bottles on her dressing table? What if she could smell out laudanum? Charlotte swirled the contents around, the syrup was thick and sickly looking. She had been tipping the syrup in every place she could fit it. First it had been a few drops in one scent bottle, and then she'd topped the laudanum bottle up with cooled boiled water from the kettle. A year later she diluted half a bottle every time she purchased a new one. The scent bottles were full of it. She held a bottle a little way from her nose; there was no smell from a distance. The scent bottles had been given to her when she was a child and apart from trying to make rose water as far as she knew they'd never had perfume in them. Replacing the stoppers and carefully putting them back she made a little sigh of relief.

Creeping downstairs she went into to the pantry, kneeled on the concrete floor and pulled out dusty empty beer bottles from underneath the bottom shelf, and right from the back she dragged out two large pot vinegar bottles. She took out the stoppers, the pots were both half full. She could pour one of the vinegar bottles into the other and use the empty one for the laudanum. Her mother hadn't discovered what she was doing, thank goodness. She should be able to save enough sixpences a week for a while yet.

Bless the holiday people. After hearing two ladies discussing laudanum while they were queuing to buy crabs a year ago in the seafront shed where she worked. She'd learned how it was addictive and could provoke trance-like states if you had too high a dosage. She'd heard them say how the doctors in London were experimenting at getting people off laudanum based products, and even removing them from the shelves, especially for the little ones, the babies, 'the quietening syrups'.

Her thoughts were interrupted by a banging on the back door. She wiped her hands on a linen towel and went to answer it.

'What do you want, Henry?'

He rested one hand on the door frame. She stepped back. Henry Card was a ruddy-faced man from all the weathering at sea, he was strong – on par with any of the fishermen, and she could see why her mother was attracted to him, his eyes were deep brown, he had a head of brown hair and long sideburns. Somehow though – he had been around for years, asking after Sally, and since Charlotte had been weaning her mother off 'her syrup' and making her go for little walks, she often appeared back with Henry on her arm.

'Yer not at The Shed then?'

She should be working at The Shed now; it was always chaos after a shipwreck, girls were late, fishermen were late with their catches, and others never came in to work at all – helping themselves instead to any salvage or just looking. She wanted a day off from severing heads, gutting and slopping innards into buckets and boiling live crabs. She'd tell them that she had to look after Will because he was running a fever.

'No,' she answered. 'Will—'.

'So yer found 'im then?'

'He took shelter in the laundry shed for some reason. Now he's running a fever,' she said.

In the afternoons after school, Will came to The Shed to write labels, and he would sort out the smallest of the crabs and lobsters and run them back to the sea in a bucket, but only the tiniest because any other small fish, slops or shellfish and fish were given to the workers as a bonus, or sold off cheaply to the poor. The fish bits were a blessing that had saved them from starving many a time since their father had disappeared.

Henry drew his fingers through his well-cut brown hair, took a deep breath and said, 'Fantasizing all night in the wash-shed. He's out-of-touch that one. He seen us scrapping on the beach trying to yank that man out the sea, he did. What did he expect, all hunker together and jolly slaps on the back. He didn't see the gaping hole in the man's head. Didn't he hear all the bells and running and knocking on doors? Look, I have my own agenda for the day, those black ponies are up and down the jetty slope all night, and now there's pickings to be 'ad. Moose-goose, I'm done here for the day. I need to negotiate any booty and it's all percentages and transporting and how much can yer salvage. I can come back by the night if she wants me? Or if the lad gets worse or needs a doctor. But you've got the captain in Will's room, and wi' Will being sick an all, yer don't want another mouth to feed. I'll eat at me lodgings. And I'll need me kip having been up all night wi' the wreck and all this searching for the lad. I'm all day negotiating. Tell Sally I'll see her anon.'

He turned and left, slapping his leg with a black flat cap. Perhaps her mother and Henry were drawn to each other because they came from out-of-town, and though they mingled and lived here, they retained a sense of being out-of-place, a feeling she'd had herself many a time.

Luckily the captain's bacon was almost done. Charlotte cracked an egg into the pan and watched it sizzle, then she laid out the captain's breakfast on the parlour table. She rang a brass hand-bell at the bottom of the stairs, and then again outside Will's room for the captain before she checked on Will in their mother's room. Charlotte stood by the door. Her mother was sitting on the bed humming quietly beside Will. He seemed to be sleeping soundly so she went to lie down on top of the covers of her bed to get some blessed rest; she eyed the brass knobs and wondered when on earth she would ever get around to polishing them.

A few hours later Charlotte was woken by what could only be her mother clattering pots in the kitchen downstairs. She didn't want to disturb this other breakthrough which was more like a miracle, so she went into the parlour to eavesdrop on her mother from a distance.

On the table there was a note, she picked it up, in neat handwriting it said,

For the boy – a shark's tooth – or a dinosaurs!
Captain O'Rourke

Charlotte picked up the fossil to feel how the serrated edges had been smoothed by the years rolling about in the bottom of the sea, it was harder than a flint stone or a brick. She closed her hand around it.

She wished the captain was here to thank him, but she knew he had left to go on some errand or secure some deal. She also knew she had to put in an appearance at The Shed and explain her absence. Then she knew her mother was at the door, watching her. Charlotte pretended to be reading the note. Moments later her mother moved away and she could smell the broth and turned to glimpse her mother carrying a tray up the stairs. Will, would be spoon-fed by his mother for the first time since he was four. Well, the vinegar pots are full this afternoon, she thought, putting down the shark's tooth for Will to find later.

Scattered fish bones, silver skins and pink crab claws littered the cobbled floor of The Shed. Deft blades cut and sliced, fish eyes popped here and there. Charlotte listened to the gossip.

'I allus wuz afread o'th storm.'

'Some say a smuggler thrown overboard in the tempest.'

'She shrook out when she saw im drowned, his feet all splaar.'

'Thars good ent it though, just the one, someone from furrin parts.'

Charlotte picked up a brush with tightly woven twigs for its head and began to sweep up the fish bits.

Through the open door she heard the clopping of horses' hooves up and down the jetty, some wood, some coal, she glanced outside, and what's that from the captains' schooner? She moved to the door and stood in awe as a merchant examined his wares on the back of a horse-drawn wagon.

Finally his mother had left the bedroom and gone downstairs somewhere, Will stumbled to the window and looked down into the alley. He'd recognised Henry talking to the man from the beach last night. Henry must have sensed Will because he looked up. Will saw him mouth the word, 'DEAD' and sweep his hand across his throat.

Will edged away from the window. He could hear his mother clattering downstairs in the kitchen. He had to make a plan to escape from Henry. Smuggling was one thing but a man could hang for murder.

The night drew in early and Will checked things in his trouser pockets, his most precious things, a small bird's skull and a shark's tooth wrapped in a large white hanky, in the other pocket, a hunk of bread and cheese in greaseproof paper. His mother was in the living room sipping her syrup in the creaking rocking-chair by the fireside. Will had dressed for outdoors, he crept to the back door determined to outwit Henry.

Chapter Three

Will imagined purple boulders instead of clouds. He heard the whinny of a horse pulling a cart and imagined it as a Horse-God and Chariot, one that could read the minds of men, slowly the Horse-God rose up with great white wings. Will moved to one side and let the sorry-looking bay horse pass, the horse's head hung low with exhaustion.

Then Will stood at the top of the jetty and imagined one schooner sailing to Iceland into erupting volcanoes, another into pirate territory on an island with trees full of oranges and lemons.

There goes the north wind again, he laughed, as it almost blew him over. He ran down the jetty, the shipwreck – for it was that already – was abandoned for the night, the wreck cried an unearthly sound.

Will would have a life at sea, rather than a death by Henry, his soon-to-be stepfather.

It was easy enough to pick out the captain's schooner with its wrapped white sails. He turned over one of the several passenger boats pulled up the beach and dragged it into the sea, climbed in, and headed for the 'Merganser'. With some expertise, considering the strong current, he thought. Waves splashed over the sides and seawater dripped down his face and neck. The schooner wasn't far. He sang the cuckoo song he'd awoken too earlier, his voice taken by the wind. His mother had sang the song over and over until he'd shouted, 'Mother, shut up!'

Charlotte stepped outside, a gale almost forced her back indoors. Sometimes, she thought, you reached the end of tolerance and something changed inside you. Like her mother must have given up a good position as a governess to come and live here, perhaps she *had* been in love with her father, and then when her father had died she'd decided to lose her mind. And now, her mother had decided to get better and look after Will. She was sure they'd be all right at home together for a couple of weeks. When she returned from her trip they'd have enough money for her and Will not to have to work in The Shed. It might be spontaneous but going to London to do business would mean they could buy a bigger house and take in lodgers proper-like.

She felt around the yard's flint wall in the darkness for the loose flint. She always thought she'd be robbed, or caught and sent to prison for her secret. But she was older now, it was time to do something positive about getting out of The Shed – take a risk.

She put her hand on the cloth bag and shivered. She grabbed the bag and checked inside. Even in the pitch black night she could see the white pearls set in rich solid gold. But they were nothing in comparison to the huge diamond set in a cluster of smaller diamonds, which was strung on the fattest, prettiest gold chain she had ever set eyes on. She put them on rather than risk them falling out of her black skirt's pocket. Her cold fingers fumbled with the catches before tucking the jewels under her blouse and her dried-out old gansey.

She left the cottage, with her mother near the fire in a rocking-chair and imagined Will was still safely tucked up in bed. She hurried by the church with its silent bells, not even glancing at the houses of the horse-clipper, the baker and the bathing-machine owner. A few minutes later she stood at the top of the jetty. By scant moonlight and lanterns on the vessels out at sea she made out a two-masted schooner, a tall-ship and a three-masted schooner. The wreck was pitching on a sand-bank at 'The Devil's Throat', she could hear it groaning.

She would take a row boat and stow aboard the 'Merganser', to London where she could sell the jewels, then, she'd have enough money to take the steam-train home.

There was a familiar cry, like the herring-gull on the church roof, so well-known, that she knew somewhere out there in the Devil's waves, was Will. Perhaps he had followed her. She was soaked with sweat even though the north wind was below freezing. She had believed Will was in bed.

'Will!' her voice was cloaked by the gale-force wind and crashes of the sea. She couldn't lose Will, not now …

'Father!' she cried, hoping his ghost might surface and shine right then. The boat rocked and all at once she was hanging onto the oars for dear life. She couldn't row a single stroke, the oars were being tugged out of her grip by the snakes in the sea.

'Will!' she cried over and over. And there he was, bobbing up and down like an apparition, somewhere on a crossroad between the Devil and her.

A powerful thing, love. She reached for the oars and grabbed them; she hung on and began to row, crying out in agony. Then, with a loud scream, by the Devil's own hand she was thrown into the air, her body flung into the hard hitting splash. The ice-cold grip pulled her down. She couldn't see anything; she was blinded by the darkness. Holding her breath she kicked with all her might and surfaced, gasping for breath. She trod each horrendous wave as it came and went. With only thoughts of Will, some strength returned and she battled with the freezing sea, she couldn't lose him, she just couldn't.

The current was on her side. Will had seen her and he was rowing nowhere, but staying afloat at least. Somehow she got within reach of him. But then, Will was thrown by the waves.

'Oh, God help us!' cried Charlotte.

Will surfaced.

'The boat, Will hang on! Help!' she cried. 'Help!'

Will clung on until she reached him. She clung to all of him, his arm, his shirt, until she finally managed to get one arm around him and the other gripping some part of the upturned boat. Will was turning blue, and his eyes were closed.

She heard men's voices.

'Let him go!' they cried.

Never. But she had no more strength. Trust in God, she thought. Trust the lifeboat men. And then everything went dark again. When she opened her eyes, all around her there was light, air, and blankets.

'Will?'

They were in a boat beside the schooner. They were being lifted. She could hear her teeth chattering. A lantern light reflected a man's concerned face. Sleeplessness washed over her, the likes of which she'd never known. It was overpowering, she wondered if this is what it was like for her mother. The glimpses for her: a group of men; a smoky cabin; Will being stripped and rubbed down; white flapping wings; a warmth from a body which cradled Will like a mother holding a baby and herself by his side; and then, a sensation of being wrapped all at once, helpless in a white cloud.

Sally found a letter from Charlotte. She began to read it. Well, she could hardly blame the poor girl. Charlotte had been caring for her and Will for six years. What was a couple of weeks away?

Sally had been wallowing and waking unchanged for these long six years, until now. Bless Charlotte, she'd even left three weeks supply of laudanum in case she was delayed on her trip. And bless her for taking Will, but she could have mentioned taking him with her in her letter. A holiday in the capital? Should she be worried? Charlotte might return with some grand ideas but that would be all. She had no need to worry about the past or anything else. Charlotte had even left three shillings, and there was another one and six-pence from last night's lodger. Plenty of money for food until Charlotte got back then, though it had been a long time since she'd cooked. There was a stew cooking on the fire spit – enough for three days. Charlotte had also been shopping there was bread, cheese, eggs and really, enough potatoes, turnip and carrots to last her through until Charlotte returned, she wouldn't have to go out if she didn't want to, except to empty the guzunder.

Charlotte had left her a lengthy 'to do' list:

1, do the laundry on Monday's
2, empty your guzunder every morning
3, go down to The Shed and tell them I've had to go away to visit a sick aunt, and get poor bags for fish stew
4, Tuesday's beat the rugs
5, Wednesday's press the laundry ...

The list went on and on. Sally folded up the note without finishing reading it. My goodness, what was the girl thinking, she could hardly move from her bed to her chair now could she?

Chapter Four

Nicholas O'Rourke turned heads as he left the alehouse at the top of Jetty Street, not only because he was the captain of the two-masted schooner but also because of his stature. He was tall and straight backed, and had an air about him of quality and kindness, at the same time he was admirable and everyone would do his bidding just at his say-so without any explanation. At the same time the busty-barmaid looked wishful at the sight of his shoulder-length black hair tied back into a pony-tail, and she had offered him his first drink free for a chance at a one to one eye-contact from his deep blue eyes. The captain declined the free offer of course and this made anyone who hadn't looked, look, and they would remember the tall captain with the dimple in his chin. Indeed he was a familiar figure in these parts, regularly transporting lumber from as far off as Canada to the quayside, and once he had caused quite a stir when townsfolk turned out to see the iron rails delivered by steam train and carted down to the jetty for his schooner and several others to 'run them up to San Francisco'. His latest delivery had caused a stir among the women-folk too. A new general purpose store had opened in the town and the store was creating a large haberdashery department. Word of the unloading of materials had spread and within half-an-hour, a crowd of women had gathered on the jetty to gaze in awe at the rich red, green, gold and blue rolls of cottons, silks, and heavy brocades.

Nicholas didn't notice he had caused a moment of silence as he closed the alehouse door behind him. In his mind he was planning a return journey to London docks and the distribution of potatoes in the cargo hold, and thinking how the crew's scrubbing and painting was soon to be in vain now that the materials had been delivered. The barmaid had offered him some under-the-counter-booty, a whole keg of brandy no less, they were trying to off-load the kegs before any coastguards got here, and it was because of the dead man on the beach. The dead man was neither from the anchored boats, nor the wreck. By all accounts he was part of a smuggling ring and the ship that had lost a man overboard had left him to his fate, or not missed him yet. They'd been using the worst of the weather to run their contraband, common enough all over the coast, yet getting more and more dangerous because of the rewards offered. How the revenue men expected any community to betray these men was ridiculous, Nicholas thought, because the folk here were not only loyal, they were most likely to be able to have things they otherwise could not afford, like the brandy. He smiled, he'd had to decline the brandy, though it occurred to him he could quite simply switch an almost empty keg he had a receipt for, for the full one. He was off to London and the excise men there were sticklers for searching, sure every vessel had something illegal stowed somewhere, and they'd probably be able to sniff the difference between brands!

'Blast!' he cursed. A dog brushed past him and he stumbled against the wall. The street lamps offered no clue as to where the dog had gone. Then he was aware of a murmuring from a group of fishermen heading for the alehouse. He hadn't imagined the dog. They made a gap through the centre of them as though they parted to let through a ghost, two of them stood edged up against the wall.

'Get a grip men, it was just a dog,' he said, striding after it.

'Stay away from that thur cur,' one of them said. 'You'll hooly cop it if yew see it. Let's hevva drink, wi' you, Captain.'

'Sorry, I have to get back. Rain-check.'

'Aye, aye, Captain.' And they laughed, one the men belched loudly, and Nicholas knew the alehouse would have no more trouble off-loading the brandy tonight.

He began to hum a sea-shanty which got lost in the gale-force wind; he heard an almighty crack and knew a mast had given way on the sand-banked schooner. He stopped humming, another ship dead, he thought, snapped like a child's toy against 'The Devil's Throat'.

And a breaker came roaring across as he turned his row boat leaving six inches of water for his waders to sit in.

A mysterious dead man, smuggling, a shipwreck, a ghost dog, treacherous seas and ice-cold north-easterly's from Siberia. He hoped the dog was a ghost dog anyway, because he didn't like to think of any man or creature turned out on a night like this. And there it was, in the sea, dear God, the poor dog was swimming, or was it a dog, was it a bit of wreck? He rowed frantically towards whatever was heading for his vessel.

'Good Dog! Good Dog!' he cried, just in case.

Through the crashing waves came a desperate reply. 'Help! Help!'

The sea was treacherous. He should not have attempted to get back to his ship tonight and neither should anyone else. Nicholas gave one push of power rowing, without fault he surged towards the faint voice. The dog must be trying to save them, he thought. And then he saw an upturned row boat riding the peaks and troughs belonging to the Devil's own throat. Was that a girl? It was too dark to tell. Whoever it was, he or she was clinging onto someone else and they were slipping below the sea. The person was holding a bobbing head above water. He pulled off his waders and stood up in the swaying row boat. For a second he was sure he was suspended on the wind before his body hit the bitterly cold surf.

He blessed his crew mates. He could hear their voices, they'd been vigilant in looking out for him arriving. He was aware of Tom in the water, the blessed strong man, his best mate. They battled the waves from opposite sides swimming towards each other and the struggling silhouettes in the water. Nicholas reached them first. The lamps from his boat were wavering up and down and he clearly saw a boy's face as he went under. Nicholas dived.

It was pitch black, and sub-zero cold. Nicholas found a hold and with a force pushing against him unlike any he had experienced before he hauled with all his might. It was the girl or boy, he or she wouldn't let go and he or she was dragging them down.

Tom, Tom, where are you?

Then they were all rising, buoyant and gasping. One more second between them and the bottom of the sea.

It was all hands and heaving. Nicholas looked pensively out across the water and asked one of his men,

'See if you can see that poor blasted dog, it's surely a gonner.'

Nicholas recognised the boy. He was from the cottage were he'd stayed the previous night. He'd been relieved the boy was well enough to be up and about at the time, he wished they had informed him about the missing boy, he would have helped with the search. From the cottage hallway he'd seen the boy find the fossilized shark's tooth he'd left, the boy had held it up to the window and examined it carefully; the boy had given the biggest sigh and clutched it in the palm of his hand. The tooth couldn't have had a more appreciative owner.

What on earth was the boy doing here on his boat? A hard life perhaps? Had he been wrong to show kindness to the boy – was he intending to stow away for a life at sea – did the boy take him for a kindly man that would allow him to leave his sickly mother? He remembered the mother, he'd seen that look many times before, the pinpoint pupils, the nervousness, the lack of appetite, the co-dependency on others to take care of them. Someone mentioned the boy's sister. This was her then. Foolhardy and reckless. Stupid and weak. White as a ghost. Hair like a wet mermaid. Limp with cold. Drowsy.

'Will?' she cried.

'The boy's safe.'

And though Nicholas was shivering and his teeth rattled, he took the blanket he was being handed and wrapped up the girl and caught her before she hit the deck, sweeping her into his arms in one movement. He let Tom carry the boy and then with super strength he carried the girl over his shoulder, moments later, he was never more relieved to be in his cabin with the warmth from a fire and lamp light.

The captain's cabin was basic with cupboards down one side, an untidy desk strewn with maps, books, papers, compasses, a couple of chairs pushed under a small round fixed table, and a hammock, there was also a small proper fixed bed for any rich passengers that insisted on one. Lamps flickered dancing shadows on walls and a small mantelpiece over the fire. Tom had already put the boy on the bed and he was stripped in seconds, he was rubbing him down as if he were a new-born, the boy was still and lifeless.

Nicholas put the girl down on the bed next to her brother. He pulled off her boots and took off her wet black woollen skirt, it was so heavy it was a wonder this alone hadn't pulled her down. He stood back.

'No time for chivalry, Captain ...' said Tom. 'There's enough of us here ...'

'Get me some hot bottles,' he ordered two other crew members. If he had to strip the girl, let there be as least men present as possible.

He slung a blanket over her and got her out of her wet clothes, he glimpsed the jewels glittering against her white throat. Was she a thief? The little mermaid was so pale, he thought, her black hair all strewn about her.

'Captain,' said Tom. 'The boy?'

The boy's lips were blue, his skin as white as the moon.

'Pass him to me.' Nicholas stripped out of his wet clothes and wrapped himself somehow in a sheet and climbed under the covers. He cradled the boy trying to use his body heat to keep the place where his heart was, warm.

'Put the girl under. Get as many hot bottle as you can and put them around the edge of the bed. Stay here though, don't leave us.'

'Captain,' Tom nodded.

Nicholas drew up the covers around the boy and the unconscious girl. He stayed awake to watch the boy's breathing and the rise and fall of the little mermaid beside him.

Chapter Five

Nicholas watched the boy, he seemed to be sleeping soundly.

Nicholas dressed in a white shirt, black sweater and canvas-type black trousers and pair of long woollen socks under his boots. He went over to his desk and opened a cupboard and poured a large brandy and gulped it down in one go. From his kit-bag he took out a striped nightshirt, something he usually wore when he stayed overnight on-shore.

Charlotte watched him through glimpses of opening and closing her eyes. So when he pulled back the bed covers she was startled but kept up the pretence of being asleep. She wondered if he could see her rapidly beating heart under the sheet. When he pulled the sheet away it was all she could do not to scream. But he didn't do anything other than pull the nightshirt over her head while pulling down a sheet so as to expose as little of her body as possible. He fumbled with the buttons down the front. Then he laid her back down and tucked her hair away from her face, before covering her back over. She sneaked another look at him and he was gathering the cooled pot bottles from around the bed. He lifted a chair and sat down beside the bed on Will's side, she could feel his gaze on her. He was probably wondering what on earth they'd been doing out there in the storm.

If he had known Charlotte was half-awake Nicholas would have questioned her about her foolhardy escapade. He had no idea the reason her chest was heaving up and down was because she had seen him almost naked, and that when he had dressed her in his nightshirt she had been so afraid and then relieved, that she couldn't move or protest.

Charlotte remembered the remarks of a young fisherman who had told her he fancied her and how he had asked her to walk out with him. She had refused, and he'd looked at her with a yearning Charlotte hadn't understood. She wished she knew more about the ways of men and women and not just the hilarious tales the women at The Shed recounted.

The door creaked open and heavy footsteps trod across the floorboards. She could smell a beefy broth. She heard a tray being put down on the table. It was Tom; he'd brought two dishes of steaming broth. The men picked up one each. And they must have spoken to each other by sign language because Charlotte knew she was being coaxed up, there was some pillow lifting and arm wrestling and she was under the captain's arm and with his other hand he was forcing her to sip from a spoon. She didn't want feeding. She opened her eyes pushed the spoon away.

'Eat, it's almost lunch time' he said, as if it would make everything all right.

She tried not to slurp for fear of embarrassing herself. When had she last eaten anything? A piece of bread when she'd prepared the captain's breakfast, was it yesterday morning?

She glanced at Will. He was taking soup from the spoon like a ravenous gull chick.

'Thank you,' she said, and stupidly, and without warning she was overcome with tears.

'It's just the shock,' said Nicholas kindly.

Charlotte was so relieved that Will was safe. She knew she could trust this man who held her under one arm and waved a spoon about in the other. He had made no attempt to take her jewels when he could have done. She looked up into his handsome face, he wasn't bearded like many of the fishermen, he was bristly skinned admittedly, she thought it added depth to his blue eyes.

'You'll have a tale to tell your friends,' said Nicholas. 'It's a great setting, Will, with the sound of the ships creaking and groaning in the darkness, the howling wind, the waves of the sea lapping, the cliffs up lit up by the moon …

You must get some rest now. I'll send someone to let your mother know you're safe, she must be so worried.'

He was unsettled with his arm around the girl.

'We don't have any parents,' Charlotte said. 'We're from the workhouse – in the city – we've run away. Please don't send us back. I can pay for our keep.' She put her hand to her throat.

Will nudged Charlotte with his elbow. And again.

'What?'

'Don't you recognise him?'

Charlotte blushed.

He laughed.

'Aye, Lass. You missed me, all night helping with the shipwreck and then looking for Will here, and then all day caring for your family.'

'I saw you leave our house,' said Will. 'With your kit-bag and everything. Thank you for the shark's tooth.' And he realised he wasn't dressed and made a scramble from the bed to find his wet clothes and Tom reassured him they were drying and he'd go and check the pockets.

'What are you children running from?' asked Nicholas.

Henry stood at the top of Jetty Street, hands on his hips, outside the alehouse. The drunks had talked a load of squit, *'That there dawg int afread o' nothing, he wuz out there, he wuz ...'*

Down at the water's edge he wondered if he should just take a row boat and head for one of the anchored ships. He looked down into the black waves, white-wash lapping over the jetty. He could make out the wreck in the distance; a mast had broken off and was floating across on the tide, flotsam for the morning beachcombers.

The coastguards would arrive anon and he couldn't rely on loyalty from the townsfolk – could he? He turned around and headed for Sally's cottage. He'd make Will understand. They'd had no choice; the Frenchie had been a gonner for sure.

The jetty was strewn with seawater, every now and then something crunched under his boots.

Once the extra drafted-in coastguards had done wi' helping wi' the searching, he'd make a tidy sum on the 50 kegs stacked in Sally's coal house. Damn the sand-banked schooner – they'd had to abandon another 150 kegs because of the attention the wreck brought down upon the town. It was a shame, the ship would off-load somewhere else down the coast for sure, and it would be awhile before they came to these parts again, searchers could sniffing around for weeks.

The boy could be trouble, perhaps he could persuade him to keep his mouth shut wi' bribery. And what was his sister doing sneaking around in the yard all the time? Was she hiding something?

He took a hand out of his pocket and tried the trick of rolling a gold sovereign through his fingers, he was slow and faulty and gave up, yet again. Maybe these last six years on a fools-gold errand hadn't brought 'im any nearer to his real goal, but he made a tidy living. He could always take the lad a walk up the cliffs. Na, stop it, what was he thinking? He was fond of the lad, Will just had to know 'is place and when to keep 'is mouth shut. The coastguards were about for sure, skulking through the alleys of a rain drenched town, looking for the damned or the chancers.

He splattered through puddles and cobbles and stood a moment to gaze up at the church roof where the slates had fallen on him giving Will a chance to escape.

He could scarcely imagine anyone working on repairing the church tower – it was so tall. Yet there were signs of clearing up, soil and flints upturned and little stacks of glass without their lead. They were having regular services on Sunday's wi' pails catching drips and boards at the broken windows. Inside he supposed the aisles and pews were all right, and the tabernacle was just a table with candelabra and stuff. He'd seen a priest wandering about on weekends, and what would the priest say if he knew 'im. Really knew 'im?

He went on his way and turned into the alley, he was tempted to check on the gallon-sized kegs hidden under canvas and covered over with coal in Sally's coal house, but he was sure he saw a slink of shadow watching from the other end of the alley.

He lingered in Sally's small back yard with a desire to bring six years of wondering to an end. Didn't the wall glitter here and there where the girl lingered and often stood suspiciously alone at night?

His hand soon became wet with all smoothing over flints and his fingertips raw with all the digging around them. Systematically he wobbled each flint stone; the wall was four or five flints thick in places. A thousand flint stones later he found a hidey-hole. Though it was black and empty, he fancied he touched grains of gold, they flicked his mind to the past.

If the father could have a so many gold sovereigns – could his daughter, who must have been ten-years-old at the time – have had some of the spoils all these years? Could she have been hoarding more gold and keeping it a secret?

He was cold from the torrential rainfall. Who'd have thought it? All this while he thought Sally was

41

the one keeping secrets, he'd never imagined the kid, the one who went to The Shed every day to skin and boil, bone and pack, who's ice-cold stare was like a scorpion saying, 'Really, you like *my mother*?' and her eyes would say, *the numb mother like a ragged doll who stays indoors and leaves us to kindly neighbours or women at The Shed*. And so he'd brought coal and sometimes tea from his booty, and sausages from the butchers, bread from the bakers, and he'd waited, his mouth shut and never-so-much as a blank-eyed kiss in return. But now, things were changing; Sally was walking out with 'im! And she called him 'Henry' like he was familiar and though he hated to admit it, he rather liked it. But the girl, she had 'im looking over his shoulder, and now the boy had 'im in such a dark place he was at ransom. The truth was he was going with the flow, piecing together what he had already said or would say if there was an enquiry at this cottage.

Children! Child, the captain thought she was a child. This bothered Charlotte more than the question he was asking. She waited for Will to speak. What was he running from? Was it purely that he wanted a life at sea and was tired of going to school in the mornings and then working in The Shed in the afternoons? She didn't believe that for more than a second. Whatever the reason was, it must be the same reason that he had hidden from someone or something the night before last.

'What is it, Will?' she turned to him. 'What were you leaving for?'

'You mean you weren't with the boy in the same boat?' the captain asked.

Charlotte shook her head. 'I was trying to reach Will, he was in another row boat.'

Will started coughing and couldn't stop.

'It's all right lad, you can tell us on the morrow.'

In the galley Nicholas and Tom took some simmering broth for themselves.

'We should send word,' said Tom.

Nicholas thought back to the night Will had gone missing. His mother had gone to bed with her syrup as if nothing was the matter, he wondered if she had known about Will being missing or if the little mermaid had kept the information from her mother. Will's sister seemed to take care of everything. Just now, she'd even offered to pay him not to send them back to their mother.

'I suppose we should, Tom. But they'll stay here until they've recovered,' he said.

He went to sit beside the sleeping pair for a couple of hours until a soft knock came on the door and Tom entered to take over the vigil.

That night Nicholas tried to sleep in a hammock in his crew's cabin. At some point he must have drifted off, but in his dreams he was re-living the rescue; in freezing water he was screaming out to reach a mermaid, her tail was thrashing the water and the black dog was trying to reach her, he reached her before the dog and swam her to a distant shore, where they lay exhausted on a beach, and when they awoke the sun was baking them, she was no longer a mermaid, on dry land they were both naked and entwined. He stirred; a growing need began to take hold of him.

A new day dawned quietly and slowly, Will opened his eyes with another coughing fit but it didn't seem so deep or painful. His limbs ached and he knew he was lucky not to be drowned. Charlotte was sleeping so deeply his coughing didn't wake her. He was glad of that.

Tom beckoned for him to come to breakfast. He crept out of bed and found on an oversized sweater, some trousers and a huge pair of woollen socks that Tom had left for him and he dressed in them and followed Tom to the galley. Tom was built like a giant, he ducked under beams as if he had hit his head many times, and unlike most sailors he had short hair, it was clean, tidy and bright blonde, his hair stood out against his skin tone which was quite tanned even though it was winter and a he had a distinct lack of any facial hair such as sideburns or beard which was not only the fashion but convenient saving you from shaving regularly on a ship.

The cook was completely opposite, he was small, bearded, with long black hair, and his name was Ed. He soon had them organised helping with scrambling eggs on a black range, and cutting thick slices of bread for Will to spread with butter.

Nicholas woke up to the sounds of a gentle swaying ship and voices in the distance. He washed in a basin of cold water, and then went to check all was well with his crew and vessel. The morning was calm enough, above them a depressing sky was covered with grey featureless Nimbostratus rain clouds. Good, thought Nicholas, no more storms today, just a potential for steady, heavy rain that might last hours, though it was cold enough for snow. He looked out across the quay, another two-masted schooner had arrived in the early hours, there seemed to be some activity aboard. He guessed it was the coastguards searching the new arrival.

The smell of eggs cooking drew him to the galley. He smiled at the scene and stood in the doorway. Will wore a gigantic sweater and rolled up trousers and was patiently and carefully buttering bread, whilst Tom was stirring eggs in a large black pan.

'Mornin', Captain,' said Will, happily.

'You're looking better.'

'Aye, Captain,' he replied.

Nicholas laughed. 'I can see Tom is looking after you. Report him to me if he doesn't.'

'Aye, aye, Captain.'

'I'll take some breakfast for your sister.'

Chapter Six

Charlotte rubbed her aching muscles as she sat up and called, 'Come in.' Nicholas carried a tray laden with breakfast. Charlotte seemed to have a heightened sense of smell because she knew he brought scrambled eggs, and they had a familiar scent like they were mixed with pepper and thyme. She wanted to say, *you have herbs on a ship*? But then she thought perhaps it was logical for those long trips with nothing fresh to eat except the fish they caught. They would dip hunks of fresh herby-bread into a fishy sauce, or make a herby-bread fish sandwich, or fried fish on herby-bread, or better still, stuffed herby-fish.

She could hear heavy rain on a port-hole from her vantage point in the captain's bed. He was as handsome as she remembered. She pulled the covers up around her, wondering if it would muffle the sound of her beating heart.

'You have a story, little mermaid?'

He put down a tray on his desk. *Child*, he'd called her last night. *Where are you children going*? She had to move, it was too late to feign sleep. Self-conscious and feeling heat rise to her cheeks she found she couldn't answer him.

'Did you steal the jewels around your throat? Does it have anything to do with the dead man on the beach?'

She started to laugh. It wasn't funny but his bluntness was startling. He might have added, *What made you so desperate to get involved with stealing and smuggling?*

'It's no laughing matter,' he retorted. 'Once,' he continued, and folded his arms, 'the sound of a cricket at night sang from a marble staircase of a hotel I was staying in. I decided to catch and release him. I swear I chased him off the stairs, around tables, around candelabra on the tables, settees; he was the quickest thing you'd ever seen. So I conversed with him, I told him if I opened the door he could just hop out. And so he did, he took off. Later when I was resting on a hammock between two trees that overlooked the Mediterranean Sea, he came back, and he sang me to sleep. I fell asleep to his song.'

'It sounds a wonderful place. Do they have chickens there?' she asked, raising her brows teasingly. She knew he was being kindly and trying to coax something out of her. But she didn't have a clue really as to what the connection was other than he thought she stole the jewels and was on the run.

'Chickens?

'Story first.' he said, nodding, realising chickens were as irrelevant as crickets.

'There is no story. Well not what you're thinking. I'm no thief.' He looked so earnest and she needed his help right now to protect Will. She decided to tell him something to keep him on her side, and so she began, 'My father saved a man's life at sea. He was asked to London to collect a medal and the man whose life he saved asked him up to his house to present him with a reward. He

47

gave my father the jewels, *for hard times or good times*, he said. It was the same place my father met my mother. She was a governess and father stayed on to get to know her. She came back with him and they got married.'

Some of what she told was true, the made up bits seemed plausible.

She continued, 'You've seen my mother. I've been working since I was ten-years-old to feed us and pay the bills, since my father went missing, presumed drowned. Mother sunk into melancholia. I need to sell some of the jewels so we can pay off our debts. I needed to get to London to do this; I have no money for the train.'

'Your father entrusted the jewels to your mother for hard times. Can't you sell them locally?'

'It was mother's idea we sell them. There's no one in town who'd buy them, though I could have tried in Norwich but mother was afraid of me being followed and robbed. Anyway, with the sale of our cottage and the money from these we might even be able to raise enough money for a large deposit on a suitable lodging house.'

The reward part of the story was not quite true, the actual reward had been monetary. The jewels had been her mothers, they were a mystery, and perhaps her mother had stolen them.

Her father had purchased the cottage and his fishing boat with the reward money. But her father's boat had capsized and he had been lost at sea and any remaining reward money had vanished with him. Although her wages would go up soon when she turned seventeen, she had to get out of working in The Shed, she just had to …

'Your mother's not been well I know that. I've seen the addiction many times.'

'I've almost weaned her clean. I heard some Londoner's discussing the method. She is quite lucid for the first time in years.'

'You've not been to a doctor before you started meddling with her medication?'

The captain was placing the tray of food on the bed.

'No. The local doctor is not familiar with the treatment. He'll catch up eventually when I'm done, when I tell him the patience and the reduction methods of the doses,' she said.

Her hands were shaking, she could hardly hold a fork.

'Here, let me.'

'No, I'm fine.' She forced her trembling hand to grasp the fork.

'Did you really think I'd give you passage to London?' he grimaced. 'The coastguards will be here in two shakes of a lamb's tail. Once they've searched my vessel thoroughly again I need their permission to load potatoes to take to London Docks. What shall I tell them about you and Will? Was Will following you – ahead of you? What was the boy thinking taking a small boat out in that storm?'

Charlotte pondered for a moment. She couldn't decide if the captain believed her story or not. For now he was okay with it. He would probably ask around in town and try to find out if she was telling the truth. But then she'd said no one knew they had the jewels. No one in their right mind was likely to spread news of any kind of hidden stash for fear of being robbed, even in their small town theft was common. And everyone was familiar with her father's story about the rescue so her story should hold up. As for Will,

'Will wasn't following me,' she said. 'He was ahead of me. He was running away from something or someone.'

'Whatever for? Something to do with the dead man on the beach?'

'I don't know.'

'He was missing all night. I can't send him back until we know his story. He's just a child. God knows what sort of danger he might be in, these smugglers can be ruthless,' said Nicholas.

'Thank you. Really kindly, you don't know what it means—'

'I have a preposterous idea. You might not agree. But we have to come up with a reason for you being here when the coastguards arrive anon. Pretend to be my betrothed, Will is your brother who you take care of, which is true. Say we're going to London to get married. Chaperoned there by my aunt. My aunt lives in my house, and you can stay for a couple of weeks and sell your jewels, then get the train back and say the engagement didn't work out. No one should be any the wiser.'

'Preposterous is right,' Charlotte laughed nervously. But they needed a quick plan and she had to protect Will.

'Can you think of anything else? Do you think you can get the truth from Will?'

'I think all he'll say is he wanted to work at sea. But it's more than that, I know it. Otherwise why would he have been hiding all night from me and why run away now? Maybe he was trying to protect mother and me. Perhaps he has been threatened already.'

'Yes, it sounds like it.'

He sat on the edge of the bed. He was so close to her she could see his chest rise and fall, she could study the dimple in his chin, knowing that a day or two ago he had shaved and now he was bristly again, that his eyebrows were the same black as his hair, which was tied back and made him look like a handsome pirate.

'I'll go along with your idea if I can't think of anything else by the time they get here. Thank you, Captain, I'm in your debt,' she said.

'Call me Nicholas,' he said. He got up and left the cabin, leaving an air behind him which Charlotte paused in before looking at her breakfast hungrily and wondering what on earth she'd agreed to do and how fast it all happened. Would an older, wiser woman have agreed to his idea so readily?

Soon after, Tom came in with a tin bath, which he filled by bringing buckets of hot water from the galley. He left dry clothes for her, a new pair of men's trousers, a cook's plaid shirt, a black woollen sweater and socks, and her own boots, which were still damp but otherwise okay.

It wasn't long before she was ready. There was break in the rain, and she stood on the deck under the captain's gaze while he pondered at the helm. It was an odd feeling being so close to a man she found attractive, her heart was pounding again and she wasn't sure if it was being near him that made her catch her breath or when he said,

'See, the coastguards are coming.'

He took a firm grip of her hand which took her by surprise and made her take a short gasp. She thought it forward of him, but didn't mind in the least, in fact she moved closer to him.

Although the two-masted schooner, 'Merganser' had been thoroughly searched, the coastguards checked the new cargo suspiciously, but to her relief they hardly glanced Charlotte's way. The cargo had been loaded, much of it in torrential rain, sack-full after sack-full of potatoes had been carried aboard and stored in the hold. The men and the five horses delivering them to the vessel had got soaked, at some point Nicholas had found four oiled canvases and went to place three of them over the black horses and one over the unloaded cargo, then he'd done some negotiation with the owner of the horses and come to an agreement for him to keep the canvases for such weather when the horses were standing about in the freezing cold and rain.

'It'll cost me,' Charlotte had heard him grumble in the galley when he was getting a hot drink and she was helping give them out. 'I'll have to replace the canvases with new ones when I'm in London.'

That had been two hours ago, now rain rippled the night, it was rhythmic music, there was pinking on ropes, whistling through un-stopped holes, a back rush of the tide. Charlotte's body said, rest, rest, but she wanted to view the lamp-light of the town from the sea, and she needed air even if it was under a drizzle of rain.

Rain had fallen in shallow pools in the worn-out grooves on the wooden deck. The hypnotic swaying boat tilted the pools up and back making tiny ripples on the surface water.

The captain had saved Will's life. She might not know the ways of men but she knew she was lucky. She liked this captain, the way he carried himself with confidence, the way he did his negotiations with the coastguards. She liked the way he must guide his vessel sweeping over the seas faster than she slid a knife under a silver skin. If it was luck to meet him, then she was lucky.

But what did he think of her really? She had told half-truths about the jewels.

'Charlotte,' his voice washed over her thoughts through the darkness. 'Little mermaid? Come inside, come below.'

She noticed his strong hands again as he helped her down and removed the oilskin coat from her shoulders. She stamped her boots and immediately wished she hadn't, it was un-womanly.

'Come and eat, Will is sleeping. We'll have to be quiet,' he said.

The desk served admirably as a table, Ed had covered it with a white cloth and silver cutlery and a candelabrum centrepiece, and he'd left a wooden trolley laden with casserole dishes and plates. Snowflakes had begun to fall outside across the quay and settled on the masts and it was endlessly drifting over the sea. Charlotte looked through a port hole, entranced.

'You would never believe the weather here, it's so changeable, 'she said. Of course he knew that. She had discovered he came to her town on a regular basis. She knew he stood right behind her. Their agreement was still open for discussion, almost as if it never happened. It crossed her mind marriage was like a job, one endless task after another, in exchange for work of another – a negotiation. Sometimes she had felt so old and responsible tending her mother and Will that the prospect of marriage to this man didn't seem so preposterous at all. She couldn't remember the last time anyone had held her and she had a sensation of being safe, before last night, when this man had undressed her and covered her over, then later spoon-fed her with one arm around her. No wonder she'd cried. It bothered her that she had lied about the jewels, but how could she tell him the truth? It was only a small lie, but one that her whole future might depend on. For he seemed to hold honesty in some regard. She gathered her long dark curls away from her face.

'Did I thank you for the clothes? The black sweater is warm. And Ed, I forgot to thank Ed for the shirt.'

'He won't mind. Let's eat. You can tell me more of your story over dinner.'

They were talking quietly; Will was sleeping in the captain's fixed bed, covers tucked right up over his ears. Charlotte sat down sideways at the desk and Nicholas served them.

'You have a bed and a hammock? Is that usual?'

'Probably not. But paying guests prefer a bed.

'Ed has done us proud.' He lifted the lid off the larger casserole and inhaled. 'He says you need feeding up, lovely beef broth,' he whispered.

Charlotte smiled, it crossed her mind if it was the same broth that the captain had spoon fed her.

Nicholas sat with his legs under the desk.

'We sail in the morning,' he said.

So it was real, thought Charlotte. London. She was sailing to London. She would sell the jewels, pay everyone on board back for their kindness and then go back home. She would like to ask Nicholas if he would come with her to do the negotiations for the jewels. But could she ask anymore of him?

'I knew a lady once who wore pearls the whole time, day and night, she never took them off.'

'A mermaid?' Charlotte joked.

Nicholas looked at her gravely, she looked down at her napkin and wished she hadn't spoken out so jovially.

'A lady with a shadow like a ghost, her tread was like snowfall and her eyes like ice-pools. I was afraid if I embraced her or kissed her, she'd evaporate in my hands. She only wore white or grey, she had hair so golden and fine. She took the same remedy as your mother. We have that in common, Charlotte.'

'Your mother! I'm so sorry, Nicholas. How long had she been taking it?' Oh the shame of her joke, how could she ever right it?

'My mother took laudanum for as long as I can remember. She died five years ago. If only we had known what you had discovered. Why did it take so long for anyone to realise it wasn't a cure but a curse?'

'What is the world coming too?' Charlotte reached for his hand across the desk, she tried to convey for him to forgive her foolish joke.

Henry sat opposite Sally in her living room, the black kettle steaming on a black ring over the open fire. He placed a silver thimble on the round oak table.

'From the 'aberdashery; for you,' he said.

'For me?' Sally picked up the thimble and examined its little humps, and then she put it on the end of the fourth finger of her left hand. 'You went into the new shop?'

'Aye. I had a wander round – curious like – it's mostly woman's stuff. Show it to the girl.'

'Charlotte? Oh she's not here. Didn't you know? Hasn't anyone said?'

'I ain't been to The Shed today.'

'What have you been doing all day then?'

'Sailin' round that there wreck, looking at them there broken planks and her hull all spread wide, and it snowed for a bit, white sprinkled on the sea, the town and the wreck, and so I came back and wandered up and down on the beach to see what's been left behind. Then I went walkin' in the town and got swept up in the commotion, in the rain then, ended up in that there new store. I was out of place but no one bothered. It smelled nice, like cheese in one room, bread in another, and you can go upstairs, and there were all these women looking at cloth and stuff, it smelled like silk in there.'

'Where is she then? Where's the girl?'

'Thanks for this, Henry. I should like to visit this shop.'

'You'll get the girl to take you, tomorrow like.'

'Oh no, she's not here. She's gone to London. Taken Will with her too. I'll have to wait till she gets back.'

Sally saw a grim look cross Henry's face.

'I shouldn't have let her go should I? They're too young?'

'How has she gone? How did she afford the fare? Why has she gone?'

'The Captain. The one that was here. The one you brought to my house. He has taken them.'

If Henry had been born to someone else, a Lord and Lady for instance, or even a fisherman and his wife, things might have been different. He might not have been forced to steal bread as a child. He might not have had to hide his eyes from the string of men his mother 'entertained'. He might not have a wonky nose where one of those men took a dislike to 'im. He might not have had to run away to sea aged eight in order to escape *God knew what* when he'd been caught by the same man wi' the gentleman's watch in the pawn shop.

He was still years on, looking for what?

A place where he didn't have to worry? replied a voice in his head.

'Work is never done, is it?' he said, and some daft idea formed in his mind that he had to go to London after them.

After Henry had left her cottage, Sally looked in the hallway mirror. It had a pretty frame, she traced spiralling stems and flowers with the thimble now on her first finger. And then she looked at her reflection, she had wanted her own house and her own precious babies. What else had she wanted? She went into the parlour and picked up the almost complete gansey, and she pulled the stitches off the needle and began to pull at the wool thread until it got longer and longer, and then she rolled the thread up into a ball of wool, then she attacked the stocking stitch until it was a pile of waves on the floor. Next was the twists and turns and the unwinding of all the knots at the bottom of the sea, she was undoing all that she had done until it was just another ball of wool. Then it was the sleeves, unpicking the casted off stitches and she was wading through rock pools, and John's face was shining in the reflections. She imagined Charlotte's voice saying,

'Not again, Mother! Not again. Make a different pattern. We could sell them on. Please Mother. Please ...'

If it was a matter of choosing, of course she chose to take care of her children. She stopped unravelling and stared at the clock face on the mantelpiece, then she looked down at her hands and at the wool strands twisted and twined on the floor. She was like a madwoman. Holy Lord, why hadn't anyone shaken any sense into her?

Will wondered what it would be like when they put up the sails in the morning and if the sight of land would disappear or would they sail down the higgledy-piggledy coastline of Norfolk towards the Thames estuary. He'd left his mother behind, she'd be wandering around the cottage, sliding from fire to chair, clicking needles, wandering down to the sea-water's edge in her pink slippers because there wouldn't be anyone there to tell her to change out of them. And would she eat? Could they trust May, their neighbour? Charlotte swore she'd asked the woman to check on Sally, *that she and Will are eating*, and she said she'd even left her some of their winter stock apples with May as payment to be sure.

And now he was listening to Charlotte and the captain, he mustn't open his eyes or blink, he mustn't cough, and he must lie still with the strong smell of broth rumbling his tummy, he couldn't even look at the rain-horses running down the port-holes.

For as long as he could remember it was his quest to learn something new every day, and every night before he went to sleep he'd go over this new thing. Today he'd learned more than one thing; the first thing was that coastguards aren't all that bad, one had tossed him an orange – an orange! And he'd yet to eat it. The orange sat on the table beside the captain's bed next to him.

He'd also learned how to store potatoes in the cargo-hold. He learned how heavy the sacks were and why the boats carrying heavy cargo didn't sink, but he'd also learned how sometimes schooners were built top heavy for speed, and why they toppled over and so many were lost sea. There was a fine line between design, safety and speed.

He learned how to whistle! Tom had patiently been teaching him all day.

And now he learned that Charlotte liked the captain and they both guessed her little brother was scared to go home. Will was ashamed of this, he couldn't 'man-up' if he was just a boy. But he knew what he had seen, and when he'd asked the coastguard if seeing the dead man's skull was horrible, the coastguard had looked at him and said, 'His head wasn't smashed in, lad, he drowned, that's all. It's a sad thing but these smugglers take a risk going out in bad weather. You'll be all right on this ship. The captain's experienced and you're on a short trip in fairly good weather.'

And now he wondered what Charlotte was wearing around her neck. Was it something to do with the smuggler and their soon-to-be stepfather? Brandy and tobacco were one thing but this was in a totally different league. He had to follow Charlotte to London, if she was involved with something bad he'd have to man-up and take care of her and protect her from Henry.

'Thank you, Captain,' said Charlotte.

'Nicholas,' he replied.

She moved her hand off his, and he put his hand on top of hers to stop her. They both stopped eating and simultaneously put their hands on their laps.

'Your father?' she asked.

'Cholera. Not long after my mother. I've mentioned my aunt – a spinster, she looks after my house.'

'Thank goodness for your aunt.'

'Yes. She's much more grounded and caring than my mother ever was. Charlotte, why don't you talk like the rest the townsfolk?'

He changed the subject. Charlotte didn't want to delve into his privacy any further; they hardly knew each other after all.

'I'm not aware that I don't speak like them. I work with them, mix with them, and have many friends. My mother schooled me until father disappeared; elocution lessons were part of it; part of her work when she was a governess. At The Shed, up until this year when the schooling law was introduced, I was allowed one hour a day to teach the little ones. Will was there too, from four-years-old up until this year when the free school opened. Even now though, he comes to The Shed after school.'

Oh please, the captain's hand had felt so strong and yet gentle, it carried an impulse which had seared right through her.

'Have you read any classic books, with your mother being a governess?'

'Yes. Mother had a trunk full of books. It was sad when Mr Dickens died this year.'

'Yes, very sad. You say you 'had' books?'

'Yes. Had. I had to pawn the books. Sometimes of an afternoon on our day off, before Will went to proper school I'd go into the little second-hand shop where the owner keeps my favourite books on a shelf. He keeps the full cover book price on them so no one will buy them. It's like he hangs onto them for me. It's a wonder in there; he has a wall of books for sale.'

'You'll like my house then. My father made a library of sorts. You'll like my aunt's additions,' he smiled.

'Romantics?'

'Romantics,' he repeated and laughed.

'My mother outlined some of those stories a long time ago; I remember her talking about them.' She wanted to add, her mother must have been a romantic because after her husband had died she just rocked backwards and forwards in her chair. If Charlotte tried to comfort her in a simple way, she pulled her hand away. The only clue Charlotte had for the rejection was when she looked in the mirror – the blue eyes, the curve of her smile, the black wavy hair, the female image of the bits of her father's face that she could remember as if she were reminding her mother of him, or maybe it was all her imagination and she didn't look like her father at all.

'Tell me more about your father,' said Nicholas.

She was having all sorts of strange new feelings since the man pulled her out of 'The Devil's Throat' and it wasn't just gratitude. An involuntary shiver ran down her spine.

'Father was alone in his fishing boat, on his way back caught in a storm. No one really knows what happened next other than the boat capsized, they think an undercurrent …'

Charlotte was silent for a moment. Nicholas ladled out broth and boiled potatoes.

Between eating she told him,

'A man came to see mother not long after father disappeared, he said we were allowed half-a-crown a week from the poor-law. Mother was in no state to work so I went to work in The Shed, thinking mother would recover. I could earn five shillings a week. I was just sorting and packing to start with. On my half-days off, when the weather was good, Will and I would catch crabs and make a few extra shillings a week. Now, we take in the odd lodger as you know. We manage all right mostly, and my wages will go up soon. It's just the cost of things keep going up, and I'm not content working in The Shed – does that sound ungrateful? I see a way of making a living with the new rush of people coming to our town for sea-air, walks and resting and bathing. I have an idea to open a lodging house. I'm good at housework and cooking, and I want to create a place where people want to come back year after year.'

'It sounds like a good plan to me. But don't get your hopes up too much. Second hand jewels are not worth as much as new.'

'That maybe the case, but we also have the cottage, and banks are lending money for new business plans.' She omitted to tell more of her secret, *I have more jewels hidden away ...*

Chapter Seven

A business woman!? *My dear your plan is impossible without a man to back you and sign the papers*! Nicholas wanted to say. But how could he dash her hopes and dreams. He'd had them once – for years he had been living his dream, and although he had been earning a wage since he was twelve it was only possible to own his vessel because of his parents' deaths and his inheritance. Yet he would give it all up and borrow from the bank if he could have his mother and father back again to tell them all the things he had left unsaid as a foolish boy and young man.

'It's a reasonable idea,' he said seriously to Charlotte. Then he imagined her in a cliff-top residence welcoming guests.

Do come in, my name is Charlotte O'Rourke. I hope you like sea-walks and lots of fine dining.

There would be a long, large hallway with a place for coats and umbrellas, a guest book on a round table laden with oranges; a parrot in the lounge (she'd leave the door open to surprise the guests). Perhaps he and Will would bring back the oranges from Spain. *Picked for you, my dear, with our own hands.* He would never do that for any other girl or woman, not the laughing girls at the inns, or the ball-gowned girls, or the Spanish Senoritas.

'How old will you be, Charlotte? Will said you have your birthday coming up soon.'

'I'll be seventeen.'

He was struck by a memory of a place between trees where the barest sunlight reached, where brambles and nettles tore and stung human flesh, where giant gnats were drawn by rotting flesh of dead woodland things, where when he stepped away, he could see the white sails on the blue sea. He never wanted to go back to a dark place.

He finished his meal in silence. Will began to snore lightly. Nicholas knew Charlotte sensed something change in him at that moment she told him her age, and he couldn't explain his thoughts to this little mermaid. He thought of the figurehead mermaid on the front of the first ship he had ever set sail in. She knew the world and the world's end, and she knew the young boy that had ran to her. *Do you mind sailing me away, Mother Mermaid*? And she had laughed, twirling her hair and singing to the wind. She showed him exotic, she showed him ice and volcanoes.

But before him, the little mermaid hung her head and kneaded a white napkin; she says without speaking, *Do you know I can't stand up because you're breaking my heart before you've taken it*? He got up without another word and left her sitting there wondering what she had said or done.

Outside, Nicholas gripped the rail on the deck and imagined most of the town was sleeping: the small cottage in the alley where Sally slept with her empty syrup glass beside her bed; the new schoolhouse where the old teacher slept in a room above the classroom which had a large picture of

Queen Victoria on the wall and a bible on the teacher's desk; the new store which had a night guard who spent the night unpacking and stacking shelves; The Shed where at night the crabs that hadn't yet been boiled alive scraped their chelae around the sides of tin baths; where a roosting herring gull hid its head under its wings occasionally peeping out from its vantage on the church tower; where snow began to fall out at sea once again.

'Your shirt is all damp,' said Charlotte, startling him. 'I could never sleep not with things how they are between us.' She brushed snowflakes from his shoulders.

He turned around. His gaze was hypnotic. His top shirt buttons were undone. 'You must be freezing, come inside, come below,' she said, fixating on his throat so she didn't have to look into his eyes.

They stood under a quarter-moon.

'You're so young,' he said. 'I thought you were older.'

'Sometimes, most times, I feel older. I've never had a chance to be young. Well, I did before father died. Since then, rarely, if ever. Young in years does not necessarily mean young in life.'

'My mother was your age when she got married,' he said.

'Did she love him? Your father? I heard not many gentry marry for love, or even desire?'

'You think I'm gentry? You know nothing about me.'

She was inches away from his face. 'Nicholas.'

'What?'

'Nothing, I'm just practising saying your name.'

'Say it again.'

'Nicholas,' she said softly, waiting for his lips to meet hers. He kissed her slow and deep. She could feel his heart beating through his shirt, his warm strong back. His hands began to wander over her, waking desires that shocked her with their intenseness.

He drew back from her and said, 'Sleep now, little mermaid?'

'Aye, Captain, but only if you tell me I'm not dreaming.'

Charlotte woke to the sound of strange voices. She was surprised by how a situation could change so quickly, one instant you could feel nothing and then the next moment, passion and a desire to be with someone. This is what the women in The Shed joked about?

She was soon out of bed and donned in the trousers and sweater which she liked wearing very much.

Up on deck the dawn was lighter, pure white snow had settled on every surface and every place: the coiled ropes; the rigging ropes and the two lifeboats.

'Morning,' a young crew member lifted his cap. He was brushing up snow from the deck and shovelling piles of glittering white overboard. Seagulls were circling and making raucous noises diving and sweeping for the slush.

A few of the other crew nodded in greeting to Charlotte as they hoisted sails. Nicholas was overseeing freeing the cogwheels and ropes that controlled the anchor. Will was watching the activity closely; he was dressed in a large sweater, baggy trousers and a pair of waders which were too large for him.

As soon as Nicholas saw her he smiled. He looked the sailor, dressed like the other men in dark, warm clothes, but he stood a head higher and more proud, and certainly more handsome than any of the others.

'How are you?' he asked, suddenly by her side.

Charlotte blushed.

Nicholas threw his head back and laughed. 'Go to the galley and get some breakfast. We have all eaten.' He put his large hands on her shoulders.

'You're not sending us back then?'

'Hell no, we sail for London as planned.'

On a tall ship, Henry gazed at the mainsail which had seen better days. He loved looking out to sea, the endless grey or blue that never stopped moving. On the deck one frozen dead eye peered out on his changing world, another dead eye looked skywards.

The great beams beneath his feet, carved by workmen, made to hold ground on the oceans was solid and safe. He held open the hatch to the cargo hold and watched the last of a sack of wheat be carried down.

They could have been orphans those kids, if he hadn't kept his eye on them. They never quite knew his contribution to their household, the coal, the bread, the cheese; the way he hung around, first putting a word in for the girl at The Shed, then visiting their mother every week. Yes, they'd known hard times, wolf just getting his paws on the doormat, but as soon as the tide turned he was there. What goes around comes around and it wasn't his penance to stay, it was his duty. Waiting patiently, and sulking into the night. And now he could see the children at a distance, they were frozen in time. And they were making 'im sail from this place, this town, for some far-off idea, some inkling of what their father said as he lay dying and clutching his chest and said, *My pockets, see my pockets, take care of my family with the rest of it.*

Henry had taken the gold sovereigns from their father's pockets and thrown the body overboard to some deep, forgotten place. Their father had been a gonner for sure, what was the difference? He had always suspected there was more gold, but Sally didn't seem to know of any, if there was a secret stash then, it rested with the girl.

The church bells were dinging and donging in some lighter mood than that of a stormy night, perhaps because he was leaving.

Le traitement d'un certain nombre de méthodes, were words that haunted Sally, what the old doctor had been trying to say was, laudanum was a method for any number of treatments, and he should have added, but it has side effects, one of them being hallucinations.

This here now, was just a slug on a cabbage. She crouched against the living room door doubled over with a memory of her mother with fifty writhing leeches about her white, sweating body, blood trickling from each wound.

'Help me,' she cried, but she knew her voice was a squeak. No one came. The children had gone to London. Henry hadn't come back after he'd dropped off the cabbages. She could run to her neighbour, May Fuller, but what could she say. How could she explain? She blinked her eyes and edged against the wall to the door, and then she ran down the hallway through the back door into the yard, and took deep gasping breaths.

It must have been the 'Fullers' hour to do the laundry. There was Mrs Fuller with a week's bundle wrapped in a sheet.

'Mrs Fuller,' she cried. Then louder, 'May Fuller, would you like a cabbage. I have a spare.'

'Dew want something back?'

She shook her head. 'It's in the kitchen.

'Yew shaking, my dear. Get yew inside.'

'I fare badly today, Mrs Fuller ...'

'We'll make yew a cuppa.'

Mrs Fuller dropped her laundry in the narrow hallway, she coaxed Sally inside. Sally edged around the kitchen door.

'Oh, you have six cabbages?' May enquired.

'Henry left them.'

'Oh, that explains a lot.'

'What do you mean, Mrs Fuller?'

'This 'ere is good tea, Mrs Mayhew, Henry charges sixpence a quarter for it, wouldn't get it any other way though. It's too expensive see, in the shops.'

No one else could see Charlotte as Nicholas saw her through the hatch below in the galley while his ship schooned the water as fast as the wind, sails billowing and flapping against the darkening sky. Gulls dropped back one by one and headed for the mainland as dusk approached. Nicholas was pretty sure no one could imagine that he was pondering on the suggestion of marriage he had put to Charlotte. And what if rumours got back to his aunt or Charlotte's mother? Would it seem like a real commitment to them and come as a surprise or a shock? Did he really care what his aunt thought? He watched Charlotte serving bowls of chicken stew with hunks of bread to his crew. She didn't know he watched her, and he noted the ease with which she served others with a smile. And Will too, taking to learning. The darkness that his sunken eyes had when he'd first seen him was beginning to fade the further away he got from whatever it was he was running from. He also saw a distinct glint of a spyglass from a tall ship, which was odd in these peaceful waters, there was a war on between France and Germany and a little part of him was concerned, he'd get Tom to check the ship out and watch if it came any closer. Perhaps someone just wanted to see who he was. He'd note it in his log anyway. Perhaps he'd take a bath and dress in a shirt for dinner with Charlotte in his cabin again tonight. Maybe he should offer her a glass of sherry. Should he ask her to wake Will up if he was asleep so she could question him? Would that be fair to the boy? The boy who hauled ropes and soaked up stories and songs like everything on board was stardust.

'And not a fish in sight,' he heard Charlotte sigh to someone. He could still feel the tingle where she'd held his hand and his quickening heartbeat every damned time she moved close to him.

Will liked the sounds that hummed and rattled through the end of broom, the bowsprit, the gaff sails, the mainsail. He learned how to manoeuvre the sails in gentle winds, learning their speed and windward ability. He learned how to handle bull ropes and tie knots in dead eyes. His hands were raw and every muscle in his body ached, but he shrugged it off as he drank strong tea with the crew and listened to their jokes and songs.

He asked the captain what he wrote each night in his log, Nicholas explained wind direction and weather, and took him on the deck at night and showed him the stars.

And even in the confines of the ship he managed to avoid Charlotte quizzing him, with a few winks here and there from his new 'mates',

'*The lad's in the middle of a knot tying lesson, later, Miss?*'

'*Not right now, Miss, the lad's learning where to tie the sail ropes, it takes concentration.*'

And he feigned 'fast asleep' again when Charlotte dined later with the captain. Charlotte didn't seem to mind too much, she kissed him lightly on his forehead and made a remark to the captain that, 'Will's cough seems so much better …' And Will learned what it was like to feel guilty and how he longed to tell her the truth. But he couldn't because of what she wore about her throat underneath a man's sweater.

The closer the tall ship got to the schooner the more Henry swayed with the tidal waters. It seemed like a chase at sea; the tall ship got closer and then fell back again and again. It wasn't luck or the wind. It was sail count and manoeuvrability. And all the while the children thought they'd left him behind.

He wasn't bitter. No indeed, he was all for change. He'd signed up for a one-way trip which was just as well given the glares he was receiving from the rest of the crew for being moody and unapproachable.

He clenched his fingers around a rope, honing in on the distance. He couldn't ever have imagined such deceit from a girl so young. She owed 'im; the slip of a girl had fooled 'im. By the time they reached the docks he'd be sure to have a plan, within two days, maybe three depending how the winds blew.

Chapter Eight

Charlotte gazed ahead at the vast and winding River Thames; they were sailing from sea to river in the early morning. They had sailed through a section consisting of three locked gates and passed a large sign that read, St Katherine Docks. What would the blessed lady have thought of these great ships unloading ivory and sugar from far-off-lands? Warehouses six storeys high blotted the landscape with hundreds of people going about their business. There were more barges than ships here than she had ever known existed. The 'Merganser' sailed on through London Docks and Regents Canal. Ahead of her as far as she could see (and further so she'd been informed) was a forest from masts of schooners, brigs and other tall ships. Many of them had colourful billowing sails from the tip of their main mast. Their sails tucked in, they hummed, sang, whistled and clanked, as a whole it was a background murmur the likes of which she'd never heard before in her own little town with its small harbour, yet the noise wasn't loud, it was something you noticed and commented on, and then became accustomed to. Into all this tall chimneys puffed clouds of black smoke into the air which hung low around the river in a grey November sky.

At first it seemed like a complete jumble of vessels, some were heavily laden and seemed sunken further down in the water. The unloaded vessels sat higher in the water and groups of them had planks from one to the other making a gangway between them to gain access to the ladders, men were unloading and hauling sacks up the ladders onto the quay.

She saw a sign that said, 'West India Docks' and 'Isle of Dogs' and knew they were slowing down and turning.

Sails were lowered. Nicholas shouted orders.

London was the furthest she had ever travelled. With a quickening heartbeat she wanted to go and help with the sails or anchor, but it wasn't a woman's place. She was in fact beginning to notice people on the quayside on the enclosed side of a tall brick wall; men sitting on any number of barrels, men coiling ropes, men talking and smoking, beggars, dock labourers fetching and carrying, pitiful-looking women dressed in rags selling sacks.

She heard orders for the anchor to be dropped, the cogs were turning; the 'Merganser' was being manoeuvred alongside a space where it would 'just fit'. She clung to a rail expecting a jolt but there was none.

'Have you ever seen so many ships, Charlotte?' asked Nicholas, appearing by her side. 'This area is designated for the fruit and vegetable markets. I have to check in with the Customhouse Officer and then go and find my merchant, then we'll unload – take the sacks through the tunnel, up the steps and into the horse-wagons.

'You'll stay here until I return.'

It wasn't an order or a request, but he gazed at her like he wanted to make sure she didn't run off, like she was young and foolish enough to take a risk. Didn't he trust her?

'Of course I'll wait here for you.'

'Good girl,' he said.

Someone behind them slammed shut a cargo hold as the smell of sewage in the river began to find her. She glanced at the dark tunnel with steps where the entrance to the city was, she could be lost in minutes.

'Come on, Will. Come away, come now,' Charlotte begged.

'No. I will not.'

'It's now or never, Will. Someone will be back soon.' It was their first opportunity to slip away in hours. The crew had gone to 'the Jolly Tar' after unloading the potatoes, and Nicholas and Tom had gone to 'sort out the finances', which to Charlotte, meant the bank. The men wanted paying, they would be back for their wages soon, and Nicholas was giving them leave until after Christmas, though some of the men were working on other ships during the Christmas break.

'We've been told to stay,' said Will.

'Yes, and we can come back. Will. Just as soon as I've done my business.'

'And what business is that?' Will stepped back from her.

The less sure she was about going, the more she pleaded with him, as if his agreement made her reckless plan the right decision.

'I can't go without you. I've looked after you all my life. Will, I would give my life for you. Trust me now.' It was blackmail that she was ashamed of as soon as the words left her mouth. 'Why won't you come?'

'Because I know.'

'What do you know?'

'About Henry. I've seen what you've got around your throat and I know where they've come from.'

Charlotte put her hand on her throat where the jewels were safely hid under the man's sweater and her own blouse which had been returned to her washed and dried.

'They've got nothing to do with Henry.'

'I saw him take them.'

'What? No, Will. You can't have. I've had these since a couple of years before father died.'

Will pursed his lips. 'I thought he might have stolen them from the dead man.'

'No, you're mistaken. Soon, I'll tell you the story about them. It involves mother. But we have to go now.'

And Will succumbed, holding out his hand. 'Promise,' he said.

'Hand on my heart, Will. Hand on my heart. I despise that man. I don't know why. What did he do, what did you see?'

Will hesitantly recounted what he had saw on the beach, and how Henry had later threatened him.

Will went with Charlotte because he trusted her. They tentatively wound through horses and carts, and horses being held by gaunt boys who stared through sunken eyes. They got caught up like sparrows among crows, they got pushed by gangs of labourers, elbowed by shoppers, street sellers shoving socks and matches pushed their wares in their faces. They paused at a baked potato seller's stall, such a delicious smell. Will dragged on Charlotte's arm as they passed a lady selling gingerbread men. They both stopped at the live birds in wired cages to stare at brightly coloured feathers. They slowed down to a leisurely pace and gazed into shop fronts stocked for sailors with navigating equipment, shirts, hammocks, sou'westers, coats and trousers, and then the other shops, butchers, bakers, greengrocers and sweetshops.

Charlotte had a few shillings in the purse she'd had in the deep pocket of her woollen skirt. The skirt had been ruined but the purse had still been there. She was grateful for it. But it was for emergencies and the purse was now buried deep in the pocket of the men's trousers she wore.

The beggars in the streets were numerous and many were children that should have been in schools by now, she guessed the law would take some time to implement the rules. But if these children didn't have any money for food why ever would they want to go to school?

She clung to Will's hand. She was in the wrong part of the city for a jeweller's shop. These big burly shopkeepers with their shifty eyes would surely rob her. She had been wrong to leave the safety of the schooner, and she was already missing Nicholas (how safe she had been for those brief moments in his arms).

'Behold! What do we 'ave 'ere then!?'

Henry's voice stopped them both in their tracks. Will's hand gripped Charlotte's tighter. Henry had a tattered appearance, not like the beggars or street sellers, but still like he hadn't slept or shaved for days. He wore his black flat cap and a dark sweater. He stood casual with his hands on his hips.

'How did you get here?' asked Charlotte, bewildered.

'The girl who never complains about her mother or the boy. The girl that cuts, boils and bones. The girl that gives nothing away and expects a few wrapped parcels for nothing. And all the while she's planning and plotting until she's big enough to disappear. And do you know what it's like for me when it is freezing and I'm sailing, and 'ere we are then.'

'What's he talking about, Charlotte?' Will whispered.

'I've no idea,' Charlotte glanced down at Will. She knew Will's secret now. She saw it in Henry's brown eyes that he knew she knew.

'Get out of our way, Henry,' she said.

Behind them a horse slipped in some foul excrement from the horse in front of it, the horse gave a loud whinny as he tried to hold his footing. The coach driver in a tall black hat shouted and began to whip the poor creature. Heads turned. Charlotte took the opportunity to run, dragging Will with her.

'Back to the schooner, Will. If I lose you, run back to the 'Merganser'.'

They ran through the noisy, crowded street, through a gang of labourers leaving the docks, they came out the other side into a road of horses and carriages.

'In here. Come on!' a lady's voice yelled from a carriage.

Charlotte hauled Will inside.

'Get down,' whispered the voice. And they crouched on a cold leather seat and heard the lady pull the door shut. She tapped behind her with an umbrella and called out, 'Drive on.'

Will regretted not having a book in the style of the captain's log so he could write down the things he learned next. Who would have thought that clouds would burst and rain would dance down carriage windows or the lady that said, 'My, that was close,' so the words could mean two things at once. Or that he dare not blink lest the twinkling brown eyes should be a vision, lest the painted rose-bud lips should not smile upon him anymore, lest the creaking leather seats should disappear before him and he is all at once in a stranglehold by Henry's thick hands gripping him around the throat.

Will swore he could smell pear drops; he'd had one given to him once by one of the girls at The Shed. He unfolded his limbs, breathless and coughing and regained his composure. His eyes widened as he examined the lady's pile of golden hair swept from her face in a bun coiled inside a ladies top hat, she was still smiling at them both. When she blinked his pulse raced. She wore a black ladies suit with a narrow red ribbon at the neckline, streamers came from somewhere at the back of her waist and these were laid out on the carriage seat so as not to crease them.

She chuckled because he was staring at her while Charlotte edged against the window to see if they'd lost Henry.

The carriage picked up speed and the horses were trotting, which given the crowded street was anything short of a miracle. The lady saw his surprise.

'If you feed the horses and treat them kindly they are always ready to go the distance for you. Not too much food mind or they will get fat! We have a very gentle coachman, his name is Humphrey.'

'The horse?'

'No – the coachman. The horse is called Hamlet.'

'Humphrey and Hamlet.' Will laughed.

'Hamlet has a small feed of corn for his lunch every day and then a two hour rest. That's how we came to be here. We were resting. And Humphrey doesn't like to be called Humphrey so we call him John.'

'John?' asked Charlotte with surprise.

'Yes. John is a good solid name don't you think?'

Charlotte didn't answer.

'Would you like a pear drop?' She offered Will and Charlotte a sweet from a paper bag. 'My name is Alice Merryweather. And what are your names?'

'Charlotte and Will Mayhew,' said Charlotte, sitting back into the seat and shaking her head to a pear drop.

'Well, Will and Charlotte may hew be lucky today,' she laughed. 'Where are you going and where have you come from? Did you steal from that man?'

'No,' said Will firmly.

She raised her eyebrows.

'It's a long story,' Will sighed then. 'I saw him do something he shouldn't have done.'

'Oh,' Alice clapped her hands together. 'I do like a mystery. Are you both in grave danger?'

'I think so,' said Will. The carriage was swaying and they were passing the shops they had idled by.

'I like to ride and get acquainted with the streets of London. We should all be acquainted with where we live don't you think? I get in my carriage with my good steeds and coachman, I shut the doors to keep out the dust and the vagabonds. You two don't look like vagabonds.'

'How do we look?' asked Will.

'Like you need a ride somewhere. Where do you want to go?'

'It's very good of you,' said Charlotte. 'It's not far. The Isle of Dogs, by the dockside.'

'No problem,' Alice said. She wound down her window and shouted directions to the coachman.

Will watched her every blink as she talked to Charlotte, he admired her high cheekbones and her small nose and chin. Charlotte wasn't wholly truthful, she said they were here to visit a family friend and they had lost their luggage in an accident when one of the crew dropped it overboard. That they had got lost while taking a walk before their carriage was to pick them up.

'But how did that man get here?'

'He must have followed us on another ship,' said Charlotte, peering again out of the window.

'Shall you tell? Shall he leave you alone if you don't tell? Have you only Will's word for what he did?' She touched her finger to her lips. 'What did he do?'

Will was breathless; he wanted to kiss her name on the water-horses running down the windows. Alice.

Her hand reached across the seat and she laid a hand on his shoulder. He crunched the pear drop.

'You should disguise yourselves,' Alice said, removing her hand from his shoulder she lifted Charlotte's long plaited hair. 'Beautiful,' she said. 'I should like to sketch you both. Do say you'll come to visit me and let me sketch you both.'

Will noticed a pencil box and two sketch pads tucked under her seat. He also noticed that where Charlotte's skin was lightly tanned, Alice's skin was white, and where Charlotte was lithe and strong, Alice seemed thin and fragile.

'The night times are worse here. Don't go out alone at night. The beggars get drunk, the prostitutes get busy, the sack-makers work by street lamps, and in it all are the soft and poor children.

'Change will take some time,' said Charlotte.

'Is it the same where you live?'

'No, it's not. The sailors get drunk and the prostitutes stay at the inns, and the children are at home tucked in bed.'

'I should like that,' she said, her excitement faded quickly and she sat back in her seat. 'Did you see the birds in their cages?'

'Yes,' said Will, eager to talk to her again. 'They should be free and in the trees.'

'In the heart of the forest,' she said.

'Aye, to the sound of the bees, wind and rain,' he replied.

'Yes, just so,' agreed Alice.

'May I see your sketches?' Will nodded to the drawing books and box tucked under Alice's seat.

'Of course,' she replied.

'There's no time. We're here,' said Charlotte.

'Then take my card, I am determined to sketch you both and show you my work.'

Will held his hand out for the card, which made Alice smile kindly.

'Thank you, Alice. We will be in touch.'

At aged six Nicholas had been sent away to boarding school, aged eight he was getting many a leg beaten before cricket, aged ten he was run ragged around fields, aged twelve he ran away from the brutes and bullies, sad to leave the true friends he had made but determined if he made it home, he would never return to the damned awful place. He took his time getting home. He walked parallel to the roads following the map he had made over the repeated journeys when he'd gone home for summers and Christmas'.

He'd read the road signs, the village names, rivers and bridges, and because he'd been on foot he was able to stop off and add other landmarks – the names of local farms and millponds. He'd laid out his map on hard stones, and ate from his meagre supplies. Often he would doodle in the margins: a kingfisher; a heron; frogs; dragonflies or a line of oaks. Sometimes at night, he'd drawn in star formations, bats and owls.

When he'd seen any man or boys, he'd hid. When he'd seen a woman or girl he had approached them and asked for food. It was just the way it was. And finally he'd knocked on his own front door and his father had answered surprised and kind of relieved at the same time.

'Has something happened?' his father asked.

Nicholas had replied, 'I'm not going back to that place. If you send me back I shall run away to sea.'

A few days later his father sent him back. Nicholas kept his word; he made his way to the docks and signed up for a life at sea. He'd never looked back. He simply sailed away and learned all he knew from a great captain who had taken him under his wing.

Nicholas understood Will. He did. Although he was younger than Nicholas had been when he left home he understood the yen for learning. What if the boy and Charlotte weren't there when he got back? What if the lad had run off again and Charlotte had gone after him. She'd promised she'd stay but the lad was her priority. He should never have left them alone on the 'Merganser'. He should have left Tom to protect them even though he'd had a lot of cash to carry.

He could hear the river gurgling, white herons in the mud banks were probing. If Charlotte wasn't on the schooner he'd be asking himself, *Did something happen to them*? She was so young – a girl. She owned pearls and diamonds fit for a queen, she dressed like a boy and looked like a princess, and she wore old boots and walked as if she wore gold slippers.

Blood roared in his ears. Most of his crew were back and mulling around on the deck.

Will and Charlotte were standing on the deck, they waved to him. He was so overwhelmed with relief that they were safe, and something else that he couldn't account for.

Around 3pm Nicholas invited Charlotte to pick up a few items from the shops to take back to his house for his aunt. Charlotte agreed instantly, leaving Will in Tom's care. She'd had no chance to talk to Nicholas about what Will saw Henry do, plus he had no idea of their escapade with Henry or of their meeting Alice Merryweather. Charlotte wasn't sure what she would tell him, she'd already lied to him about the where the jewels had come from, how could she tell him she'd done something so stupid as to venture into the streets with no idea of where she was going, the situation made worse by taking Will along.

Nicholas didn't speak much in the carriage other than to say it wasn't very far. He seemed preoccupied and stared out of the carriage window. It gave Charlotte a chance to look at what women were wearing more closely. They passed shops with dummies dressed in clothes much like what Alice had been wearing, hip length jackets and overskirts. Some had plainer tailored costumes and overcoats more suited for the colder weather. There were also dresses made of materials and colours in deep greens, blues and gold. The shop windows were adorned with gloves, hats and scarves. Charlotte was self-conscious as she stepped down from the carriage in the trousers and baggy sweater, she still had her long plait, the well-dressed woman and girls she saw all had their hair done up in a bun or ringlets. Tall, handsome Nicholas wore a loose fitting brown woollen suit. It soon became apparent that no one really took much notice of them, and actually she wasn't half badly dressed compared to so many labourers and poor people milling about.

They chatted briefly about the different classes of people that intermingled before Nicholas stopped in front of a milliner's.

'You should have some proper clothes if you're coming home with me, my aunt would never forgive me if I tell her we lost your clothes overboard and I didn't replace them.'

'I can't repay you, not until I've sold these.' She put her hand to her throat where the jewels were hidden.

'We'll see. Let me do this small thing for you now.'

'What will your aunt say when you turn up with us. What if a rumour has got back to her about the tale we told the coastguards?'

Nicholas grinned. 'Don't worry. I'm sure it won't have. Let's go in.'

Charlotte agonised to pick out one dress from so many. She knew she should have to have a crinoline which stuck out behind to make a bustle. She chose a dress of deep blue, its skirts dropped over the bustle and ended in a short train, it was low cut at the front and had lace trims. It was the most beautiful dress she had ever seen. When Nicholas seemed distracted getting advice on purchasing a tweed suit for himself and a grey skirt for her (the latter which she could change into), she brought knickerbockers with one of her own shillings. To finish off Nicholas purchased her a pair of high, soft black leather boots which buttoned up at the sides, and a grey cloak which could be worn with anything. He wanted her to have more but she insisted they stop to buy woollen trousers and a jacket for Will. Nicholas got the few things his aunt had asked for and they left the shop loaded with parcels.

'I will pay you back, Nicholas, I will.'

'What if I don't want you too, what if these things were a gift. I've enjoyed your company so much.' He took a deep breath as if he wanted to say more, but instead he nodded to a tea shop. 'Ever been in one of these?' he asked.

'Not yet.' She laughed.

He opened the door and a rush of warmth hit them with smells of coffee and cinnamon. A young girl in a brown dress and cloak, agonised at the long counter which was spread with sandwiches, iced cakes, almond biscuits, chocolate macaroons, cinnamon cakes and various tartlets. The girl's mother, clad in striped brown outfit shouted at her to sit down, so that everyone in the shop turned to look. Some women were accompanied by men, some were alone and some were in pairs. A waitress in a blue frock and long white apron showed them to a small round table with dainty chairs in a corner by the window. Nicholas put the parcels in a pile on the floor and pulled out a chair for Charlotte. She thought everyone glanced their way, for Nicholas was a handsome devil and they must have been wondering what on earth he was doing with her. Still, at least she was wearing the grey skirt he'd brought for her, and she slipped off the grey cloak reluctant to get it creased on the back of the chair or hand it over to the waitress. She decided to keep it on her knee. When she'd been changing she had quickly coiled her hair up under a brown hat, she patted it now, knowing wisps of her hair were in her face and hanging loosely down her neck.

'Would you like afternoon tea?' the waitress asked, much to Charlotte's relief. She would have been rather like the young girl, undecided what to have.

'Thank you,' said Nicholas for them both. 'That would be lovely.'

After she'd gone he said, 'They close in an hour, it's been a busy day.'

'Yes,' she replied. 'How different it has been from back home. How quickly we adapt to our surroundings.'

'And how quickly we get used to each other's company,' he said with a smile and added, 'I should like to buy Will a book to write in, and some pencils.'

Yes, he was a good, thoughtful man, thought Charlotte, as they tucked into sandwiches with fillings of eggs pounded with butter and cream, and afterwards scones with butter and blackberry jam, served with Indian tea. While they were eating she told him what Will had seen Henry do that night on the beach, but she didn't tell him she'd gone off looking for a shop to sell her jewels or of their chance meeting with Alice Merryweather. Nicholas nodded gravely at the story involving Henry.

'It was pitch black, in a storm, Will might have mistaken what he saw. It must make it terrifying for him. He wouldn't want to send a man to prison, or worse, nor would he want to let a murderer go free. It's such a dilemma given the man's role in your lives. I'll talk to Will, get him to go over the details with me. I'm disappointed that I was in your house that night and didn't know Will was missing until the morning. I would have helped you look for him. I'm sorry I wasn't aware.'

'I didn't know you then,' said Charlotte.

It was dark outside, someone was lighting the street lamps; inside the shop lanterns were being lit.

'We always knew Henry was involved with smuggling. It actually made our lives easier. We might have starved if it weren't for him. To be honest I don't think Will would ever tell on him. Henry could never be sure Will wouldn't tell though.' Yet oddly, thought Charlotte, Henry had seemed more interested in her when they'd come upon him. He couldn't have been watching her could he? He couldn't have seen her remove the flint stone in the wall and remove the jewels could he?

That same afternoon when the rain stopped, Sally stood at the leaning gate to the church path. Where the ancestors slept, the gravestones moved, and though her pulse was racing she decided it was such a short path there was no need to go around them or abandon her idea. The ground was wet and puddles reflected the church walls and the grey sky. It was a clear run over the uneven path and she had her boots on. *Shopping* the lady of the manor used to say, *was exquisite.* My, she looked at the heaps of rubble on the church ground, nothing ventured – and she was off, her goal just the other side of the path and over the road to the new shop where the haberdashery was. She who goes shopping shall have some new wool and a pattern. Mrs Fuller said the store had knitting patterns. She crossed the road and went in through the door, a bell tinkled. Given the store was on three levels and divided into different departments on each level Sally thought the bell frivolous or a relic from the previous building. She didn't want this area, it was ornaments and clocks. She went up the first flight of stairs. This is what they talked about, rolls and rolls of materials, a feast for the eyes and the textures of those velvets imprinted on silks! There were so many delights, but she pushed on to the wool section. Mrs Fuller had been right, there was a tome of patterns divided into sections, men, women, boys, girls, babies and other. She turned to the boy section and chose a grey pullover and went to buy the wool.

On the counter was a small dish of pale pink and yellow sugar-coated almonds.

'Please take one,' said a young girl assistant. 'They're for our customers. You're Mrs Mayhew aren't you? I know your daughter, Charlotte.'

'Oh, that's nice, dear.' Sally told her what she wanted and paid for her purchases. She held the paper bag and its contents with such pride. 'How do you know Charlotte?' she asked.

'She regularly comes into my father's shop with Will on their afternoons off. She helps him with reading. Sometimes I sit in with them. I would never have passed the exam to work here if it hadn't been for Charlotte.' The girl passed Sally her change. 'I must say I was surprised to hear that Charlotte was getting married. To that handsome captain, what a catch.

'Mrs Mayhew? Mrs Mayhew are you all right!'

Sally came round in a chair, in a new place with a steaming cup of tea in front of her, someone was adding sugar and stirring.

'Charlotte's away. Perhaps she's not been eating,' the girl assistant suggested to a portly man.

Sally breathed slowly and deep, she ate a biscuit and drank her tea, she cracked a sugar-coated almond and dribbled. But she couldn't talk, she couldn't answer questions. And when she recovered a little she went home with her paper bag full of wool and a pattern, she walked back over the church path with her head down and didn't notice if the gravestones were moving or not. All she could think was, *I must go to London. I have to stop her.* The captain left an address in 'the signing in book' Charlotte insisted they had. *If we take in lodgers, Mother, we have to do it proper. If we have an address and they do a runner we can trace them.*

94

Dear Charlotte, she couldn't marry a sailor, what was she thinking? Look what happened to her father, she didn't want that for her girl.

Baked potatoes were a treasure indeed. Henry purchased two. He headed after a mudlark that he'd seen creeping between people. He found the boy folded on the ground by an iron-fenced wall. He crouched down to the boy and shook him awake.

'Here, lad, fill your belly, and take these.' He also gave the boy a new pack of six cigars, knowing the boy could sell them on and maybe the boy might not have to wallow in the river's stench for a day looking for anything discarded.

'Why aren't you in school?'

The boy didn't answer, he was already scoffing the food and pocketing the cigars.

'I guess you're too old for school, eh?' Further along the fence were two girls similarly clad and covered with dry mud. Henry was filled with pity, when he looked further he could see boys holding horses' heads, boys selling evening newspapers. Over by the lamplight older girls and women were using the light to sew sacks. They were mostly silent and they reminded Henry of when Charlotte was reading. She'd been lucky that one, a proper job, a roof over her head, and all the while she had stuff she could have sold on. She would rather have let her little brother and her mother starve rather than part with whatever gold sovereigns she had been stashing. If it hadn't been for 'im they'd have starved. She owed 'im, she did.

He headed for 'The Jolly Maid' pub, surprised it was still there and looking pretty much as an eight-year-olds memory could recall. His mother used to work from the pub, years ago. She was probably dead by now but he'd have a drink and make an enquiry, she'd been sixteen when he'd been born, same age as the girl was now.

A horse drawn carriage moved through the dark streets of London, cocooned inside, Will drifted off to sleep. Charlotte dwelled on the closeness of Nicholas. She wondered if it was crazy to be with him and went over in her mind how she had got to be here. Was she taking the easy way out by being under his protection or was fate playing an ace card? He reached for her hand as Will dozed; she was beginning to trust Nicholas rightly or wrongly and the idea of them being together sat comfortably with her. She would have liked him to kiss her again, to remind her she hadn't been dreaming that he had kissed her.

The horses and carriage left the narrow crowded streets into wider empty streets; gusts of wind caught the carriage and rocked it. She immediately fell into the comfort of Nicholas's arm; she was against his ribs, his heartbeat pressing on her ear. They were travelling together yet they hardly spoke when they should have so much to say, she didn't speak lest she should disturb these precious moments. She sunk into sleepiness. What could the future hold for them? Perhaps he was just looking out for them and as soon as she'd sold her jewels on, he'd go back to sea.

She had seen another type of poverty in London. Compared to many women and children she and Will were well-off. She had a job, Will too, and ever since she'd had a job she'd been able to keep all her wages and manage the house. No one questioned her mother's ownership of the house. If they'd been in London they might have been thrown out years ago and the house passed on to some random lost relation. She wasn't aware they had any relation to speak of, which was just as well because it meant there had been no one to fight over the house. The law had changed again this year, so her mother would now legally be able to keep her property, which meant she could sell it. But would her mother go along with her idea now that she was becoming more lucid. Would her mother want to leave the cottage and risk some half-planned idea to move into a larger house with accommodation for several guests?

Will could soon earn as much as an adult worker at The Shed, though Henry had offered to take him out fishing and pass on his skills so Will had a trade. But that was before the storm, the wreck and the dead man.

What did Will want to do anyway? How could a ten-year-old decide his future?

Will still hadn't eaten the orange he'd been given. He'd put it in the paper bag with the notebook and coloured pencils Nicholas had purchased for him and tucked the bag safely under the carriage seat. '*I don't want the orange to lose its colour*,' he'd said. And he'd thanked Nicholas a hundred times for the notebook and crayons.

In a gust of wind branches swept across the carriage roof. Nicholas peered out of the window then looked down at her, and all at once she knew the tenderness of his kiss on her lips again.

She wanted the pleasure to be endless, to be wrapped up and warm, to be safe yet imperceptibly changed forever. She was retreating into another world, a new world, something beyond world.

Will stirred.

Nicholas stopped kissing her and looked up.

'Will. Go back to sleep, we'll be another half-an-hour yet,' he chuckled.

Charlotte shivered she was losing heart and faith the closer they got to his house and his aunt. His aunt would never approve of her, a sixteen-year-old who worked in The Shed for a living. Perhaps she would be right not to approve. This handsome, rich adventurer could marry any woman he desired.

They arrived.

'Welcome to Summerville House,' said Nicholas.

Charlotte could hear a dog barking from inside. Will woke up as soon as the carriage wheels stopped turning and the horses made little snorts. He reached down for the paper bag under the seat and clutched it to his chest.

Charlotte had been so preoccupied with how she was feeling she had overlooked how this must all be for Will.

'Will, everything will be all right,' she reassured him. 'A few days here in this wonderful house as guests and my business will be done, then we can go home.'

Will nodded, but looked like he didn't believe her.

Nicholas looked at her with that grave expression he'd given her when she'd made the joke over dinner on the 'Merganser'. The look was fleeting and she wondered if she'd misread it.

They stepped out into the dark road. Here and there she spotted a gas-light, but too far away to light up the frontage of Summerville House.

Nicholas guided them through a walled iron gate and up a gravel path. Her eyes adjusted to the dark and she noticed the tall trees, the neat lawns, the tidy shrubs. The house cried exclusiveness. Its solid stones grew lighter the closer they got. The frontage had five large windows, two on the ground floor either side of the door. The door was grandeur, built into a porch and hallway. There were smaller windows in the roof, and two round port-holes either side of the middle window above the door. They were like eyes peeping down on the new arrivals.

She hadn't expected this elegant house and as if Nicholas noted her hesitation, he took her hand and led her up two steps to the door.

He knocked loudly. No one answered so he knocked again.

'Don't you have a key?' Charlotte asked.

'I don't,' he said. 'Don't take one when I'm away.'

Then the door opened.

'Nicholas!' cried a lady of about fifty. She wore a grey dress and a full white apron, her hair was in a bun under a white cap.

'Mrs Johnson! How are you?'

'Well, my dear.' She embraced him, kissing him on both cheeks.

'This is Charlotte, and William, Will for short.' He stood back and introduced them.

'Well. My. Welcome. You will be staying with us I presume. Come in, come in. I can't wait to tell you about this one. What an adventurer. Your Aunt Mary was so pleased when she heard you were coming, Nicholas. But still, you're here now, you can explain all about your guests …'

They had stopped in the hallway. The coachman brought in their packages and Nicholas' bag and left them inside the door. Then a little black terrier dog came leaping and bounding from inside the house.

'Skip, you naughty dog, you've escaped!' The dog was jumping up Will, who immediately put his bag down and started fussing the dog.

It was a reprieve for Charlotte and Nicholas. They had agreed they would explain the truth to Will about the marriage proposal and the reason for it as soon as they got the opportunity, but what would they tell his aunt?

Mrs Johnson was taking off Charlotte's cloak. Charlotte had to let the cloak go this time, the beautiful soft grey cloak, and her brown hat. Her hair was a mess, pins and grips hastily put in hours ago were poking out here and there, she could feel them when she patted her hair, and the plait was unwinding.

'Come inside. Aunt Mary is in the drawing room waiting for you.'

They entered a well-lit room, two gas-ceiling lamps with six white shades each, lanterns standing on an oak panelled piano which also had brass candle holders hinged to it and various other candelabra with lit candles burned in the room. Aunt Mary was standing eagerly awaiting them. Charlotte's immediate thoughts were how short she was, she wore a long-sleeved green dress and a loose wool shawl. Her hair was streaked grey and blonde, her brown eyes scrutinised her over a small nose.

Charlotte thought her heartbeat must sound louder than the ticking of a grandfather clock as she stood wondering what to do when the aunt held out her hands and walked over to her before greeting her nephew.

'Welcome, my dear. You must be freezing and tired after such a long journey. And who is this young man? My little Skip has abandoned me already!' she laughed.

Mrs Johnson came in and set a laden tea tray down on a round table covered with a red and green damask cloth.

Charlotte found herself sipping tea from a white and brown stippled teacup. She glanced around the walls adorned with artwork, and a large gilded framed mirror over the blazing fire, a sideboard glittered with silver objects, but most luxurious of all was a wall-to-wall thick multi-coloured Indian carpet.

Will had gone out of the room to play fetch and catch with Skip in the hallway. The aunt chatted away to Nicholas but it was a quiet conversation and Charlotte found she couldn't hear what was being said.

All of a sudden Aunt Mary turned to her directly and said, 'I am surprised, shocked even, to hear the news. It's not what we had planned for Nicholas. Anyway, how old are you, Charlotte? You seem so young.'

'She's nineteen,' interrupted Nicholas.

What was he saying? He continued the charade and lied to his aunt?

'I, I,' she stammered. 'I'm really tired. It has been a long journey.

Chapter Ten

Charlotte closed pink brocade curtains and sat on the end of a bed which had pink pillowcases and sheets, and a rose-pink down quilt three inches thick.

Her plait tumbled down when she took out the pins and grips. A thoughtful Mrs Johnson had left a hair brush on the dressing table. She brushed the knots and tangles from her hair and looked into a mirror over silver candle-holders. She wanted to hear Nicholas creak along the landing and knock on her door, explain what he was doing and saying to his aunt. Was he telling lies about her age and their relationship just so she could sell her ill-begotten goods in London and then make haste for home or was there more to it? Did he truly have feelings for her?

And what should she sleep in? She decided it was best to hang up her new outfits in the good-sized oak wardrobe. There were more parcels than the dress and suit Nicholas had purchased for her. She unwrapped brown paper and found there was also a long white nightdress, two white blouses and a brown skirt the same as the grey one she liked so much. It couldn't have been a mistake, they would never have fitted his small and portly aunt. Nicholas had been thinking of her, making decisions without discussing them with her. It was all going to be so expensive. She didn't know how much she'd get for her jewels but any money she got would disappear fast at this rate. She might even end up with nothing. Then she'd have to make the trip all over again to sell more ill-begotten jewels.

She got into the nightdress and wondered if this was what it was like to be a real lady, climbing into bed exhausted from the shopping and dining out. She wanted to check on Will and explain to him the marriage proposal with Nicholas had started because of the coastguards and they were trying to protect him, but she was too weary to move. She listened out for Will going in his room, which was next to hers at least. It sounded like he had the dog with him. She ached for Nicholas and lay awake for an age tossing and turning, plagued by broken sleep and rethinking the events that happened to her and Will.

Will put his precious parcel on a dressing table and scanned the room. He tried the mattress out and to his delights it was bouncy and had several blankets so he could layer them to whatever temperature he chose. The room had a man's wardrobe and when he opened the door he was amused to find one side had drawers with little brass labels: undergarments; socks; ties; handkerchiefs. It was as if someone had thought a man might muddle his clothes up.

He went back to unpack his parcel, and empty his pockets and lay out the things on the bedside table, a fossilized shark's tooth, an orange, a notebook and crayons, a pencil sharpener, a card that said, 'Alice Merryweather portrait artist, with her address underneath.

He unpacked his old clothes, his new clothes, and changed into the nightshirt Charlotte had worn on the schooner. He wondered how Tom was, alone on the schooner, guarding it, thinking about essential maintenance. Will would have liked to have been with Tom to learn more. Still, if Charlotte was really getting married wouldn't that be something to write about. He decided to start writing in his notebook, but where to start. What if the notebook should get into the wrong hands for someone else read about Henry? He decided not to write about Henry and to start with the morning he woke up on the 'Merganser', and make a list of what he had learned about boats, with added coloured drawings. It would take him several nights and days! He was about to begin when he heard scratching at the door, joyfully he let Skip in. The dog jumped on the bed and sprawled out waiting for his tummy to be tickled like he'd done it many times before.

'Okay, Skip, you can stay,' he laughed.

Downstairs on a round afternoon tea-table were untouched fruit scones, butter and jam, a half-empty tea-pot and a dish of the curious cubes of sugar, Nicholas had held one between his finger and thumb.

'Nice. They had these in the tea shop,' he said.

Nicholas looked at the furrows on his aunt's forehead. He was grateful to her, for looking after his house, for the care after his parents had died, and she had been someone to come back too, someone else who would remember and talk about his parents. Yet here she was now warming her tiny hands by the open-fire.

'I take it she doesn't come with a dowry?' she cleared her voice like the words had drained her voice.

'Aunt?'

She blew out the candles in the silver holders on the mantelpiece.

'Don't you have a candle-puffer for that – some gadget?'

'I mean – what do you know about her? How long have you known her? How could you possibly? Are you bringing her here to live?'

'Aunt, your place is here until the day you die, nothing will change here. I promise you that.'

'Everything will change.' She went to pick up her teacup, but stopped short, gripping the hard back of a dining chair. 'And what about Alice? she added in a high pitched voice. 'What about your promise to Alice Merryweather?'

Henry stared out of window of his room for the night in the pub, he pondered on the beggars and thieves hunkering down in the dark, flocking together for safety. During the day they had boundaries, honoured them, honour among thieves and beggars, if they didn't fights, would break out, stabbings even. There was some lee-way when it came to the young uns, they would be taken under someone's wing. Whatever, most remained homeless once they were homeless, they'd enter the streets and the docks and wonder and wander endlessly. Yew needed a head on your shoulders and a bit of dare-devilry to get out of it. Yew couldn't be afraid of the sea or anything else, especially hard work. Yew needed to keep your head down and not falter, think of new landscapes and keep dreaming, even if yew were lying on a hammock with twenty other men coughing and snoring while the sea above raged and thrashed the ship. Yew needed to keep a half-open-eye for any skirmishes and not take sides, and later, when chances came, yew had to grab them with both hands.

So how had he come to be almost settled then? How had he taken the safe route these last few years? He'd created opportunities sometimes, but he'd never meant to settle. He hadn't planned it. He couldn't trust anyone, not even a slip of a girl that had 'im fooled all these years. She must be laughing her head off.

Men stumbled out of the door below him, he could hear the slowing down of clopping horses and carriages.

The flickering gas lamps moved over shadows on the curtain-less windows.

He wrapped up in a grey blanket, there was a cold breeze through a cracked pane. He was tired out, and for a moment he thought of his lodgings in Cromer and the chequered curtains at his window, a blazing fire in the hearth on cold nights and clean fresh sheets on his bed every week, the way his breakfast was laid out for him of a morning, the neat little covers on the back of the dining chairs. He could say, 'it was pleasurable', like home comforts. And what about Sally, with the kegs of brandy stashed in her coal-house? What had brought 'im from there to this? The girl – sneaking to London trying to outwit 'im? There was spontaneity about his actions; this had always been his downfall, act first, think later. He was too stubborn to backtrack. What he started he had to finish. And the lad with eyes like a spyglass – the homely little kid that raced crabs down the beach. He was fond of Will, he was. Will reminded 'im of 'imself when he was a lad, except he had never been so lucky, never had proper opportunities. Will should be grateful and supportive. It must be his sister that had put Will up to this. What was she up too? What had she been hiding that she had to come all this way to London for?

The next morning, Nicholas said to Charlotte, 'I'll show you around the house, and later we we'll go and find that clergyman to marry us.'

How could he continue with this game? thought Charlotte, and she tried to give him the same grave look he gave her when she said something he didn't think was appropriate. Nevertheless, she followed him as he strode quite proudly around Summerville House. The basement had a large fully equipped kitchen, which Charlotte loved instantly and would have spent some time helping and chatting to Mrs Johnson as she went back and forth to the dining room with breakfast dishes, but Nicholas led her enthusiastically towards other rooms which led off the kitchen, a utility room and servants' quarters, three small bedrooms which were used for storage (what a waste, thought Charlotte, they could take in lodgers), and a sitting room. Nicholas explained that apart from Mrs Johnson they had a cleaning lady come in three times a week and she also helped with the cooking when needed. Charlotte wondered how they managed with such a big house, but he explained his aunt usually dined with Mrs Johnson and did little entertaining. They went back upstairs.

'The drawing room you saw last night, come ...' he led her through a door on her right. Charlotte gasped with delight. It was a library with mahogany shelves filled with wall to wall books she couldn't wait to explore. A large mahogany desk domineered the centre of the room and there was also a couple of comfortable-looking settees.

'How wonderful!' she cried.

'I've spent many happy hours here,' he said proudly. 'But come, we haven't finished yet.'

On the same floor was a grand parlour adorned with green walls and velvet curtains, carved furniture, a matching lounge suite, and a huge fireplace.

Another door led to the main dining room. The twelve-seater table was still in the process of being laid up for four with silver cutlery and breakfast china. On a dresser, breakfast was almost ready, a fruit bowl, bread and butter and covered silver serving plates.

'We've about ten minutes, come.' This time he took her hand as if it was the most natural thing in the world and pulled her up the stairs.

'Aunt's room,' he indicated. 'Mrs Johnson's at the end of the hall.' He pushed open another door. It was his room. She could smell the manliness of him and his soap. There were several books on his bedside cabinet, his kit-bag on the floor beside a double wardrobe. She walked over to the window and gazed down at the grounds, the lawns and tree lined borders.

'I don't think it's appropriate—'

'Summerville House has three acres of grounds. There's a hidden vegetable patch behind the privet hedge. We have a gardener one day a week.'

'Do you miss your parents?' she asked him.

'Sometimes. I left home when I was twelve. Before that I was sent away and cared for by strangers. I was put amongst those who appalled timidity, often mistaken for the shyness it really was, or simply not knowing how to behave in a given situation. It was a childhood of not showing emotions, and learning when the opportunities arose. It's a touchy subject for me, three of my friends consistently beaten to their souls over the years, eventually I wrote to their parents, fortunately their parents were sympathetic and my friends were withdrawn from the school. The situation made me a suspect and a target though. There was only so much I could endure. Ultimately I was a boy among men-bullies. I'm not someone who is timid, Charlotte, but there is a rule if you want to survive. So that's when I ran away to a life at sea. I was twelve.'

Charlotte held his hand and they stared out of the window together at the little birds fluttering around the branches and a red squirrel holding a pine cone leaping onto a pile of logs.

'Has he told you anything of his secret?' Aunt Mary asked, lifting her head slightly as if it were a matter that should be revealed.

Charlotte had a forkful of scrambled eggs and was just about to eat it. 'His secret?'

'His secret,' Aunt Mary repeated with some satisfaction.

Will was tucking into ham and eggs and a large chunk of bread and butter. Nicholas was giving his Aunt Mary that grave expression Charlotte had come to recognise, he also took a deep breath.

'Yes, he had a wonderful childhood. The best school, yet he chose to run away when he was twelve. I mean what sort of boy from a home like his chooses to run away?'

Charlotte was sure Nicholas breathed out a sigh of relief. He stared at a cut-glass jar full with blackberry jam when his aunt spoke.

'It was quite common back then and now if truth be told, eh, Will,' he winked in Will's direction.

'It broke his mother and father's heart. They had high hopes for him. A lawyer maybe, like his father.'

Charlotte wanted to reach out to Nicholas; his aunt had no idea what he had been through as a child.

'A boarding school gives you more to think about than an education, Aunt. If you're unlucky they can break you,' Nicholas said.

'But you aren't broken are you? I mean—'

'It's Charlotte's birthday tomorrow,' chipped in Will. Silence fell on eight empty chairs and three other occupied ones. 'It's a special day because our mother won't be here. She's always been here for our birthdays even if she was – you know. If I'd been at home I would have made a birthday cake.'

Aunt Mary seemed taken aback, she looked as though a new bright idea had entered her thoughts.

'We can make a cake together, Will. And we can have a dinner party tomorrow night to celebrate. How would that be?'

'Wonderful, thank you, Aunt.' Will smiled.

'No problem.' She patted Will's hand.

Charlotte could hear the pit pat of butter as the aunt spread butter on bread.

The mind is full of dark matter, thought Sally. She knew it was morning by the light around the curtains, and she knew there wasn't a gale because she would be able to hear it, yet here the curtains were again, billowing, reaching out to her like sails in the wind. She watched them for a minute, the way they'd settle and then ripple, wave after wave. It was never easy in the morning. Worse now. No Charlotte to get her out of bed, no Will coming in with his blonde hair all tousled, and his absorbing smile.

She was occupied in that waking space where the mind is nearly free, when the influence of events come pinging in one a time. Will had been sick, was he still sick? Charlotte had given up the ghost on her; indirectly her daughter was making a stand.

Time to get yourself together, mother.

Charlotte wasn't a sad girl; she sometimes sang and hummed of a morning. But by the time the dark crept in and the horses heads began to hang low, she'd be gazing into nowhere, thinking too much. Charlotte had a purpose in mind, there was no doubt about that. But when Sally thought about it, when had Charlotte even met this captain? Had they met in the night under her roof like secret lovers?

She got out of bed and moved over to the curtains. The curtains were still. The mind plays tricks. She smothered a laugh. Henry had not been round since her children had gone. She hoped Charlotte was all right – not got herself into trouble, not *lost her way.*

What a fanciful thought she'd had yesterday. Sally Mayhew catching a train and going to London! The very idea!

There was a murmur in her head, not a voice exactly, more like a listener, someone listening in on her thoughts.

'What do you want?'

The truth? Oh Lord Almighty, there it was. So now she had to protect herself from the wild boar that galloped across her thoughts sticking its horns in where it pierced something painful.

The truth! it snorted.

'I shall not bring trouble to this household!' she scolded it, and with that she drew back the curtains and let in the light. She would wash, dress, eat and begin the new knitting. She set about tipping water from a jug into a bowl and splashing her face. She remembered Charlotte's list of things to do. She had to make a fire or stoke a fire or build a fire? First she had to fill the bucket from the coal house. Should she do that before she got dressed or eat first? Damn the girl, she didn't leave an order of things. Damn the voice, it wasn't listening.

Sally shovelled coal until she hit something with a thud, like wood, that stopped her. She'd always suspected Henry of using her coalhouse for storing his ill-begotten goods. A bit of delving and rummaging revealed his booty hidden under shoddy sacks. She spent an age covering them over again.

'What yer doing, Mrs Mayhew?'

Couldn't the man see, she was shovelling coal to fill her bucket?

'You must be freezing?'

She must look a fright, her arms were smeared with coal-dust.

'You shouldn't be out this weather in your bedclothes? Let me 'elp, Mrs Mayhew?'

She looked down on herself. A white nightie now streaked with black, a black shawl and pink slippers.

'Thank you, Coastguardsman. What's your name?'

'Is Henry not looking after you, Mrs Mayhew?'

'My children have gone to London. Henry is missing.'

'Missin'?'

'Can you carry my bucket inside?' She put it down on the floor in front of him and shut the coal-house door.

'Have you reported him missin'?'

She turned the large iron key and gripped it tightly. 'He often doesn't come to visit for days at a time.'

'Shall I make enquiries for you, just to be sure?'

Sally put her hand to her mouth. All the world was spinning. What was he inferring? The thoughts of Henry missing at sea had never occurred to her. Her knees gave way and she knew the ground was coming up to meet her.

Chapter Eleven

Under the grey sky their tongues had stopped wagging for sure, thought Henry, taking in the cemetery of unmarked graves. On the borders creeping between the hardened ground blackberry bushes threaded and weaved tendrils that quite beautifully, hung frosted dried dead-ends over the dead. He had a number for his mother's grave and he found the spot, he was pleased in a way that his mother had an end position, so she had a marked path next to her. Blackberry bushes spread under a willow tree, and over the wall, a field, where trough and furrow blazoned with white diamonds, where during the seasons there'd be men with heavy horses, and there'd be green, then gold, and now the crows were cawing in the morning, here and there were toadstools, red, white and cream ones, all glittery and holding their ground; it was all kind of comforting.

He stood for several minutes blowing on his freezing hands and wondered if his mother had given him much thought over the years before she'd died. He wondered if she'd ever expected him to return home – if you could call one room home. She would have said, *Little Moose Goose, run down to the offi and bring me my medicine.*

That's where he got the saying from! Those little words that slipped between his tongue and his mind like a foreign body in his mouth, he fancied he slapped his leg a little bit after he said them.

Perhaps now he remembered the words would slip away from his repertoire.

He'd ran off to sea and never come back.

He imagined his mother would say, *Got a card once – from France of all places. Fancy that, my Little Moose Goose, got a stamp and evertyhin'. Comment ça va?*

Isn't he clever, my Little Moose Goose'

'Je suis bien, Mère. I am well, mother.'

He had no flowers.

He went to seek the groundsman or the clergyman, to enquire about a headstone, put one of those gold sovereigns to use at last.

Charlotte sat in the library, it was mid-afternoon, and she was doodling on a sheet of paper at the large mahogany desk: How To Cook Fish, by Charlotte O'Rourke; 250 Fish Recipes by C.M. O'Rourke; Simple Fish Recipes by C. Mayhew; Ways With Sea Creatures by Charlotte Mayhew.

She'd also been reading, 'How to clean bird cages', which told not only how to clean the cage but also the birds as well. It also said, 'Do not be afraid to get soap in the bird's eyes and mouth.' She imagined using a badger-hair shaving brush and lathering a pretty love-bird from the street hawker, she foresaw the bird trembling and coughing, and then dunking the poor thing in a bowl of clean water. Would it blink? Would it still be able to fly? Then she thought perhaps it wouldn't matter if the caged bird was clean and pretty.

A faint knock on the library door was followed by Will entering.

'How have you been getting on with the aunt, Will?' she asked him.

'Okay,' he said. 'I've come to share my orange with you.'

'Oh, thank you. That's very kind.'

'Not at all. I wanted to talk to you about something.'

'Me too. I have some explaining to do.'

Will pulled up a stool meant for standing on, and he sat opposite Charlotte at the desk.

'You look nice in your new things. Are the trousers itchy?' she asked.

'A little.'

Charlotte pushed the notepaper she'd been writing on for Will to peel the orange on.

'That's a good idea,' he said, reading what she'd written.

'I've been day-dreaming,' she said. 'I should have told you something really important, Will. I never quite had the right opportunity.

'Nicholas and I, well, we're not really getting married.'

Will looked like he was attempting to get peel the orange in one long length while he digested the information. 'Really not?' he asked.

'Really not,' she answered.

'But why?'

'Because he wanted to keep us safe when the coastguards came aboard, he said it spontaneous-like. I feared for you, Will, I surely did. I didn't know what you'd seen or what you were running from, so I went along with his idea because it seemed like the right thing at the time.'

'Spontaneous-like.'

'Aye.'

'I've been making a birthday cake with the aunt, she likes baking. She really believes you intend to get married, or at least that Nicholas has proposed. And she thinks you're going to be twenty-years-old. Here …' He put half an orange between C. O'Rourke and Ways With Sea Creatures.

'Remember last Christmas, when Henry dropped off a bag of oranges for us?'

'Yes, he said it was *spontaneous*.' Will raised a smile.

'And we took two and sat on gravestones to peel them. We scattered the peel to share with the dead.'

'Spontaneous-like,' Will added.

'Aye, and we joked about the jealous eyes of gargoyles.'

'Aye, the herring gull began screeching.'

'And you threw him a segment.'

'Aye, and he caught it and swallowed it.'

'Aye, aye,' Charlotte laughed. 'Can you keep it secret, Will, until I've finished my business here.'

'I do trust you, Charlotte. I'm disappointed you're not getting married though. I like Nicholas.'

'There's something else though. While I was beating butter and sugar and the aunt was sieving flour and Mrs Johnson was cracking eggs, the aunt told me she's invited some guests for your birthday dinner. Charlotte, they've included Alice

Merryweather and her family. It sounds like they know them quite well.'

Charlotte closed her eyes for a second and swallowed, the orange left a bitter taste.

'What else have you been reading?' asked Will, picking up one of the several volumes on the desk. 'Lost treasures of Great Britain.' He put it down and picked up another. 'Navigating Britain's Coastal Waters by N. C. O'Rourke. Charlotte?'

'Yes. It seems Nicholas is also an author as well as a captain.'

'Can I read it?' Will asked.

'I should think so. But don't get any orange on it.'

Will wiped his fingers on his trousers then eagerly turned a few pages. 'Have you seen—?'

'Yes. I'm just trying to take it all in.'

'It says, 'Illustrations by N. C. O'Rourke and A. Merryweather.''

Charlotte nodded. 'I know.' She took a deep breath. 'A. Merryweather – I'll bet no one knows she's a female except the publishers.

'It only means Nicholas and Alice know each other,' said Will earnestly.

'But she's so talented, and rich, and beautiful.'

Nicholas sat in a barber's chair in front of a round mirror. The barber was applying lather with a badger-bristle-brush. He remembered Will watching him shave on his vessel. 'Haven't you seen anyone shave before?' he'd asked.

'I guess not.' Will had replied. 'Maybe I did when father was alive but I can't recall.'

Nicholas viewed himself as others might see him. The man who sailed in all weathers and all seas, the man who could not change tides but sailed with them, cutting his boat through the waves, his crew slowly letting out the sails, and he, watching land disappear or appear, as if the boat was making decisions, or the wind, or the night stars as they arced round and about.

He pondered on his aunt's words: 'Has the girl bewitched you?' He wasn't seeking love and neither was Charlotte. Perhaps out of the chaos of the sea that night the sea gave her up to him. *Here if you can catch her, she is yours.* He thought of her hand reaching to him on the deck. This is what touched him the most, it was what, 'turned things'. A girl standing on a boat and instinctively reaching out to him, so he took her hand and he'd had an overwhelming sense of belonging, as if it were meant to be. As if these people outside putting up umbrellas to shelter from the rain were like ghosts echoing on the streets while the rasp of the blade cuts across his chin. Behind his face in the mirror he imagined he saw his father standing lonely in the drawing room as if his world had emptied into the sea. Nicholas had never understood his parents' relationship; it seemed to him like his father had never quite caught his mother in the first instance. Like they had drifted around each other, first his mother held out her hand and his father never caught it, then his father holding out his hand and his mother letting it slip past her. This is the difference with him and Charlotte. The firm grip. He caught her and she caught him and they both held on.

In the mirror's true reflection he thought he saw a familiar horse and carriage trot by, the barber caught his gaze and stopped cutting, and for a second they both turned to look outside through the glass, and all the horses and carriages were moving slowly in a downpour, coachmen pulled their tall hats over their faces and turned up collars of their mackintosh's and they ceased shouting. It was hard to see if they were solemn or drenched. The horse and carriage he thought he'd recognised was just another horse and carriage.

He thought back to when his aunt had said, 'What about Alice Merryweather?' He had looked at her gripping the back of a chair and replied, 'What about Alice?' in a deep voice.

He swung his chair round and the barber raised a cut-throat razor, its steel edge glinting in the flickering lantern light.

Outside standing on the docks, Nicholas drew in a sharp breath of foggy air, he looked along the river at the number of boats and ships. No matter what time of the year or the weather it was always a haunting sight. Although the fog was creeping and crawling, it was patchy and stayed low. The masts of the grand ships stretched as far as the eye could see around the river's bends. He stood by the wall where the steps led down to the docks, below him on the gangway a couple of sailors were smoking and talking, ropes and barrels at their feet; across the short bend in the river a small barge had docked, its large iron anchor was laid simply on the concrete path, its thick rope wound around in a bobbin style, someone skulked against the wall, a beggar or thief, and four men were mulling around the barge not really doing anything at all, it was still life, yet busy, and made all the eerie by the grey light. This was a scene Alice should draw for reference for the future, for he feared that this way of life would trickle away now that the day of the steam engine and the railway had arrived. At some point he'd have to sort out the 'Alice' problem. He wanted to tell Charlotte his true feelings for her, but he had to tread carefully so as not to shock Charlotte with his sudden burst of reality, he didn't want to just jump in, in case she didn't feel the same, but he'd seen her look at him and he was sure there was a deep connection between them.

He ran down the steps and hailed Tom on the 'Merganser'. Tom stood on deck as if instinct had brought him out from whatever he had been doing to know that his captain had arrived. Tom was the most solid man he had had the luck to employ. Other men would be off and take to the inns and ladies of the night, but not Tom. Tom was content on the 'Merganser', he never tired of a life at sea. He knew without Tom the decks would be slippy, the sails would be in need of repair, the underside would be full of barnacles and whelks. If Tom wanted he could take a job on any of the tall ships or clippers and set sail for longer voyages with warmer climates.

'Tom,' he nodded. 'I've secured the coal run for three months starting January.'

Tom nodded.

'It'll be hard graft and possibly freezing.'

'Wouldn't have it any other way,' replied Tom, and shook his captain's hand.

In the library the evening drew in quickly, Charlotte closed the curtains. She knew she should attempt friendliness with Aunt Mary. Nicholas hadn't returned from 'his negotiations' and Charlotte began to rationalise that he would most likely not return until very late.

'Not at all,' said Aunt Mary. 'He won't be home tonight. Didn't he tell you? He has a business to organise, merchants to see.' Charlotte thought his aunt grimaced through a row of yellow teeth with at least two molars missing. 'Charlotte dear, you have so much to learn about Nicholas.'

They were at the dining table, there was beef, potatoes, parsnips and cabbage. Food seemed abundant in this house. She found she could hardly eat any of it, the beef was too rare and rich, the potatoes oily, or perhaps she was tense because Will was like a little god and more sympathetic to Mrs Johnson's cooking trying to please her with his ravenous appetite.

Candles were burning in the centre of the table; light from the flames lit up a bowl of wrinkled apples. Charlotte thought someone should bake a pie – make use of them.

'They'll go outside for the birds,' said Aunt Mary, catching her glance.

'I could make a pie with them,' said Charlotte.

'They're not fresh enough.'

'I'd love to have a proper look around your kitchen and your range. Will you show me how it works? Can I see your pots and copper-based pans? Can you ask her to show me how to make this divine sauce?'

'You like to cook?'

'Yes,' joined in Will. 'Charlotte does all the cooking at home.'

'But I only have a spit and a small fireside oven,' added Charlotte.

'She makes amazing things with fish,' added Will. 'And she can dress a crab better and faster than—'

'I should be delighted to show you my kitchen,' interrupted Aunt Mary.

Charlotte was glad of the interruption even though it was rude, she feared Will had been about to say '*The Shed*'. What would this woman have made of that! Aunt Mary had paused from eating and put a small finger on her lip as if to say, *perhaps this girl has something after all.* Charlotte took a sip of water.

Mrs Johnson came into the room and went to the fire to stoke the red embers. She didn't speak and Charlotte wondered how long she'd worked here, waiting on this small woman who looked after her nephew's house. How monotonous the daily chores, days of opening and closing curtains, making fires, beating rugs, cooking for two, three times a day, falling into bed alone each night with no one else but an extra cleaning/kitchen lady three times a week to talk to. Was she lonely? Did she just get on with it and count her blessings? She looked at Mrs Johnson's fingers for a wedding ring to be sure. Mrs Johnson seemed to be at the heart of this house without any recognition. Yet perhaps she was content. Mrs Johnson caught her eye and smiled kindly at Charlotte's gaze as if to say, *If I'd been pretty or born to gentry, things might have been different, but I've come to know my lot and accept it. I'm grateful for it.*

'Can I take your plate, Miss Charlotte?'

Charlotte nodded politely. 'Thank you.'

'Do you sew, Charlotte?' Aunt Mary asked.

'Yes. I'm quite competent with a needle.'

'I'm working on a countryside scene, it's very complicated, a tree, a badger, a squirrel, you know the sort of thing, there's even a little bee.'

Charlotte had misunderstood, her sewing was crafting, turning a man's shirt from the pawn shop into one that fit Will, or patching cotton squares onto the one thin tablecloth they owned or re-hemming curtains so the tatters and the faded parts didn't show. It hadn't always been this way, she remembered doing cross stitch as a child when her mother taught her but now it seemed so long ago.

'Mother is good at knitting,' said Will. 'She knits ganseys. I've never seen anyone knit as fast as our mother.'

'Well I can't knit at all,' said Aunt Mary. 'I should like to try. Could you teach me, Charlotte?'

'Of course,' answered Charlotte. She could hear the wind gusting outside; she imagined what it might be like at the docks whining through all the ropes.

'Mrs Johnson would you be kindly and take Skip out tonight after our dessert. I don't fancy going out in this storm.'

'May I come too?' asked Will.

'Of course,' Mrs Johnson winked. 'I'll wait for you in the kitchen.'

After meringues with preserved raspberries and fresh cream, served in blue and white china dishes with silver spoons, Charlotte held a spoon and peered at her odd reflection. How could Nicholas do this to me? He wouldn't return tonight, she thought. He'd be out at an inn pouring ale down his throat and eating pear pie as he made arrangements to sail coal back and forth during the cold months to come. She had to pretend she knew how to cross-stitch and herring-bow with his aunt. She had a vision of his aunt's tiny hands and grinning yellow teeth while trying to teach her casting on and wrapping wool around, hoping the wool didn't sag or snap, and all the time those unspoken truths rattled in the wind and spat in burning logs.

She cleared her throat and sipped more water. She'd managed so far this evening without

Nicholas, she could do a few more hours, and the room was well lit at least.

'Do you have knitting needles?'

'Oh no, dear, we should have to buy some, and a pattern perhaps? I believe it's 'the in thing' to use a pattern nowadays. Tonight I thought we could read.'

Charlotte tried not to let out a sigh. 'And could you tell me more about Nicholas' book?'

She added the 'more' so his aunt didn't know she had had no idea Nicholas was an author.

'I can dear, I can. It all started when he was a small child, he drew pictures of the garden, can you imagine, measuring and scrawling all those calculations, what a brilliant …

Sally remembered how no man ever stepped in unison beside her, they always seemed to be one step ahead – John striding to the horse and carriage which brought them all the way to Cromer almost seventeen years ago, he'd opened the carriage door and turned to wait for her. She thought of the awkwardness between them when she climbed inside the carriage with a tiny bundle in her arms.

Always, when she'd followed John along the beach, he pressed on – always something else on his mind, she would stop to pick an unusual pebble or to watch the sea, weighed down by a child on her hip, small arms clinging on.

And Henry? Sometimes when she took his arm, it was as if he was pulling her along impatiently, especially up slopes. She often thought he would disappear altogether, like he was waiting for something else to materialise, he'd slap his cap on his thigh and go striding off into the world.

Now, the coastguardsman had returned and told her Henry had gone to London, working his passage by all accounts, then the man suggested, 'Perhaps also the chance to watch over your children? Perhaps to earn some extra cash for the wedding? *Surprised he didn't let you know he was going, Mrs Mayhew.*' Then he'd looked at her oddly and suggested she might have forgotten.

She'd waited a moment or two for the back door to right itself and the coastguardsman to disappear.

Mrs Fuller – May – her neighbour and friend stood by the window rolling a pebble in her palm. She was the best person to have around right now because she put the pebble back on the windowsill and went to make tea. And then she sat down in the other chair by the fire beside her, sighed, squeezed her arm and said,

'We all get confused, Sally. Perhaps Charlotte told you and you didn't hear her properly, and that's why she asked me to look in on you, but it was you that came across to me and I'm glad you did ...' May rattled on about self-pity and the school teacher, but Sally only heard the odd word. Sally was thinking her neighbour was second-best at home, second-best to a boat, a bar, a hoar, and she eats too much and talks too much. But Sally knew what it was like to be second-best, you could never quite believe how you got there, or how you thought you could change someone. A lifetime later in spite of the beautiful children you shared, it left an ache inside that was similar to self-pity, but wasn't, nor was it lack of self-worth, it was an ache that came from being second-best or last-best and sometimes not even any-best. Then, when you realized that fact again and became determined to do something about it, some event, some little gift or act of caring, would reinstate that condition where you thought you were moving up the list of importance, just enough to stay, just enough to start dreaming and making new plans again, or to find yourself with child and making the best of things again.

Charlotte must never be second-best, never that, never second-best to the sea. She had to warn her, make sure she didn't marry this stranger until she knew she would never be second-best. She interrupted May, who was still talking about something at the school.

'Mrs Fuller, May. Will you help me pack a small bag and get the train to London tomorrow?'

'Really? Really! You're going to London on your own in your state?'

'State? What state?'

'The laudanum, Sally. You know it spaces you out. You've been a bit better lately. More lucid. Perhaps you've been taking less of it, but whatever you do don't stop it all together at once, they say you get terribly sick.'

In the back garden of Summerville House, Mrs Johnson said, 'Aunt Mary's not a bad person, Will.

She means no harm to Charlotte. It's a confusing time for her. Charlotte turning up out of the blue like this.

'There was someone else, you see, there may be still. Nicholas has yet to give his aunt an explanation about this other person.

'I probably shouldn't be telling you all this, Will.

'Do you think we should tell Charlotte before these visitors arrive tomorrow for dinner? It is her birthday after all and none of this is her fault.'

The rain had stopped but thick black clouds hung above them. Will had a sensation of being brushed all over with prickles. How was he supposed to make the decision she asked of him? Should he tell the truth that Nicholas and Charlotte were only pretending they were getting married? It was unfair to these people, it was unfair to—'Is it Alice? Is it Alice Merryweather?'

'Indeed it is, Will. But how did you guess?'

He knew in his heart it was Alice. He couldn't tell Mrs Johnson how he'd met Alice or how she'd rescued them from Henry. 'Do you think the news about Nicholas and Charlotte would break her heart?' he asked instead.

'I don't know, Will. Sometimes I think these planned things are so wrong, other times I can see the logic in it. Those two like each other well enough and they work well together.'

She called out for Skip, and he came running back to them, shaking his little black terrier body from the residue of rain he'd gathered on his coat from the bushes.

They went back indoors and Will went to his room. Nicholas was man of his word and Will guessed or hoped that there was more to it than what the elderly woman said. Otherwise it might be his fault. This had all started because of him. Nicholas and Charlotte were protecting him. He might be responsible for breaking Alice's heart all because he couldn't man up to Henry.

He did the maths. Alice was twenty and he ten, she'd consider him a child. If he were twenty and she thirty, she might regard him as a young man. If he were thirty, rich and well-travelled, and she forty she'd be only too glad to marry him. He couldn't wait twenty years. Perhaps fifteen then? It was a hopeless dream.

Skip was making little growls on the bed; he was flat out on his back again, as if he were trying to cheer him up.

Will picked up the sharks tooth. He could not believe Nicholas would betray anyone – especially not Alice. The game his sister and Nicholas played was fooling everyone, perhaps even themselves as they were clearly besotted with each other. When Alice and her family turned up tomorrow on Charlotte's birthday of all days, how would Alice react? Would there be shouting and perhaps Alice's father might even strike Nicholas. And all for what? So Charlotte could carry out some secret business that might involve smuggling or worse.

She said he should trust her.

He put down the sharks tooth and picked up Alice's card. He'd seen a book in the library, 'The Streets of London', he'd traced the map he needed on a sheet at the back of his new notebook. He knew roughly how far her house was from here and he would go to see her. He needed to find out the truth about her and Nicholas, and if it was true about their engagement he would explain how Nicholas and Charlotte were protecting him with their folly.

The last time Will had crept out of a house without telling anyone resulted in him nearly being drowned and taking Charlotte with him. This time he should be safe enough, though he had probably underestimated how far Alice's house was. But he was committed now, and he should be back by the morning and no one would have to know he'd been gone at all.

They were strange streets and roads to him, and he'd drawn on his map where he thought he might make short cuts. He wished he had a friend with him, someone to talk away the chill of the night, maybe someone to tell him to go back. Then he saw a creature standing in the dark misty road. A bay mare whinnied as he approached her and she came forward to greet him. He put his hand in his pocket and held out a sugar lump, the horse's mouth tickled his palm as she ate it; he stroked her head with his other hand. They heard voices in the distance and the horse pricked her ears, flicked her tail and slowly walked away with a soft clip-clop into the night's fog. It never occurred to Will to ride her or catch her, he thought she was on her own journey and they were two strangers meeting in the night.

He decided to walk on the pavement next to the hedgerows of the grand houses where he could be invisible and crouch or leap over wet prickly leaves should he have to escape. Sometimes, a leafless tree dangled its black fingers over him, to drip or investigate his new cap.

Sometimes he stared to a distant bedroom window, alert for a candle or lamp. The chill of the night crept further around his throat, so he turned up his tweed jacket collar and pulled down the sleeves of the old gansey he wore over his crisp new shirt.

The second creature he met was a fox. The fox froze on the spot when he scented Will. The fox had been walking light-footed along the top of a neat square box hedge. He stared at Will. Will thought the fox was possibly hoping he was camouflaged. Will stared back; he noticed hunched bony shoulders, how the fox's whiskers gathered droplets of dew, how a fox's scent smelt strongly of a pungent nettle patch. Will reached inside his pocket for another lump of sugar. Startled by movement, the fox leapt into the garden of the house he was stealing from, Will threw a sugar lump over the hedge and it fell sparkly white into a dark grassy patch.

The third living thing Will came across was when he sensed he was being followed. He swore he heard the rattle of an oilskin coat as if someone lifted their arm to his cap or re-positioned his hands in his pockets.

It wasn't a search party. Charlotte would not know of her brother's whereabouts, she wouldn't know he was gone, not yet, not with pillows under his blankets making him look fast asleep by any lamplight from the doorway. Will decided at that moment that Henry, was actually, very clever, that Henry, could probably find a dead blackbird in the dark, under a mile of hedgerow, and that he should have anticipated that Henry was in London for him, and that Henry, would never let a sleeping dog lie in case it woke up with him unawares and the dog sprinted up to bite him when he wasn't looking.

Will slipped through a gap in a hedge at a point where a block of privet had been shaped to a bird. He breathed in deeply and out slowly. He had to be like the clever fox. Slip into back gardens and creep from one to another. Keep an eye open for any lights in any windows and for any barking dogs. He thought of Nicholas and his maps, how Nicholas might map these gardens with two pieces slowly moving amongst them. He hoped he slid across the fences and hedges squares away from Henry. He knew Henry would be moving somewhere and Will knew that at some point he would slip off the squares and that Henry would remain, flummoxed and alone. He also knew he could no longer go to find Alice's house in case it endangered her. It occurred to Will that months might pass or even years, and he might spend a life at sea and never see his mother or Charlotte again. But then he saw himself changing into a man, and once he was strong, he'd come back and face Henry, man to man. He'd be reunited with his sister and the woman he loved – Alice Merryweather. So right now he'd make for the docks instead. Find a boat or ship like Nicholas had when he'd been a boy. He'd follow a different route on his map which had several churches clearly marked and would help him find his bearings.

What is love between a man and a woman? thought Charlotte. Is it changing in this modern world? The working class had no problem with it. Love to them was a solid thing. It came on the wind, rain or sun, it was simply there and acted upon. The upper class relationships between a man and woman, well, that seemed to be all planned, nothing to sing about, lives rooted in money and title, dry throats with so much to say and no one to say anything too.

She was walking on a web of deceit. Nicholas was everything she had ever dreamed of or imagined in a man. But really, she was deluded. Nicholas was merely looking out for her and Will. Events had gone on to take a complicated turn.

Old ladies in striped dresses and yellow teeth were dismissed as if they had no right to the truth. Ladies who drew in eyebrows and invented complicated relationships yet never had any of their own.

She could hear his aunt playing the piano and singing: 'Gather ye rosebuds ...' His aunt had quite acceptable singing voice, if a sarcastic one.

Charlotte was at the top of the stairs and couldn't quite hear the rest of the words to the song but she could guess them.

She had to speak to Will. She couldn't slip any further into this charade.

She tapped on Will's bedroom door.

He was asleep? She went into the room uninvited.

Will had the covers right over his head. She looked for his little nose peeping out of the blankets with the light from her candle.

'Will?' she whispered and gently shook the covers until she realised he wasn't there.

Aunt Mary was playing piano downstairs now. Skip had been barking at the back door on and off for an hour.

Charlotte was aware she was shouting.

'WILL, WILL!'

The household fell quiet. She was panicking because of the last time he went missing, the dark moments came flooding back to her. She took deep breaths and looked around the room for clues.

The shark's tooth was missing, so too was Alice Merryweather's card. Will's notebook was still on the bedside table so wherever he'd gone this indicated he hadn't intended to go for good or he would have taken the notebook too. Charlotte opened the notebook to the last page Will had been writing.

Plan for drawing lessons with Alice

1) *The London Railway Stations (or just Kings Cross).*
2) *The Houses of Parliament.*
3) *Trafalgar Square (Nelson's Column).*
4) *The Vegetable Market*
5) *The Horse Stables at Camden.*
6) *Pen and Ink Portraits.*
7) *A variety of Sea Shells (visit the Sea Shell Museum).*

In return

1) *How to fish with a line and hook.*
2) *How to fillet and cook the fish.*
3) *How to make papier Mache puppets*
4) *A trip to the seaside and rock pooling*
5) *?*
6) *??*

Flicking through the rest of the notebook Charlotte discovered the last page had been torn out. She remembered Will had spent some time in the library tracing his pencil over the street maps of London, and repeating out loud Alice's address.

'Will's gone,' she said without turning around, she had heard Mrs Johnson and Aunt Mary dash up the stairs and enter the room.

'Where has he gone this time of the night?' asked Aunt Mary.

'I think he's making his way to Alice Merryweather's house.' She sighed with relief because at least she had a destination to head for.

Charlotte heard Skip pound up the stairs and with a little yelp he leapt onto Will's bed.

'Goodness,' said Aunt Mary. 'Does the boy let the dog sleep on his bed?'

'Does it matter now? The boy has taken off somewhere in the middle of the night,' said Mrs Johnson.

'Well, get him back then.'

'Shall I fetch a carriage?'

'Yes, yes, do that. I shall go to bed. It's past my bedtime.' She turned her back on Charlotte.

'Will is confused, Aunt Mary.'

'Confused,' she heard the woman mutter. 'What's a boy got to be confused about? All this fuss. He'll be back when he gets cold.'

'That's what they said when Nicholas took off,' said Mrs Johnson.

'Well go quickly then before he gets too far.'

Charlotte gathered her long skirt and sat on Will's bed. Skip crept onto her knee.

'Don't worry, Charlotte. I'll have a carriage here in half-an-hour. We'll look for Will together. Skip can stay with Aunt Mary. He's been barking and growling at the door for about an hour, so I figure that's the start Will's got on us. If Will has gone to the Merryweather's house we'll soon catch up with him.'

Charlotte pulled the neck of her grey cape together at her throat and watched Mrs Johnson turn a large iron key in the front door.

'There,' she said, and took a deep breath of the cold night air. 'It's been a long time since I had an adventure,' she said.

Indeed her cheeks were rosy after going out into the night and rushing back with the carriage. She was dressed in a dark maroon cloak, and instead of a hat she had wrapped a similar colour shawl around her head, neck and shoulders. Charlotte wished she had worn a shawl too as Mrs Johnson buried her chin into the woolly fabric. They climbed into the carriage with just a glimpse at the coachman and two sturdy black horses. When she was working in The Shed Charlotte always ventured out with an excuse to say hello the horses and the man at the reigns. 'Where is this batch off too?' she would ask, and they would joke back, 'Iceland!' or 'Siberia!' and they'd laugh, because of course the packed fish would be heading off to hotels or the fish market 25 miles away. Recently though, orders were also being sent by steam train to the London fish markets. She should like to visit the London fish market. It wasn't on Will's list but perhaps he would go with her and not Alice?

The coachman had been curt and polite. A tall-hatted man that looked straight ahead.

Moments later they were being driven to the Merryweather's house. Charlotte gazed through the carriage window trying to memorise the route, so if she were alone and lost, she could retrace the roads by the houses and winter trees. It was nearing midnight, it was dark with only an occasional glimpse of the moon. After about fifteen minutes the coachman cursed and yelled and pulled up the horses.

She saw a red fox dart from under the wheels, she was sure she saw his tongue lolling to one side as he turned to grin at her.

'Poor thing,' said Mrs Johnson.

'It's all right,' said Charlotte. 'It's run off into someone's garden.' There was no sign of Will. Charlotte was aware of an emptiness inside her, if he disappeared and ran away to sea as Nicholas had done, she would never forgive herself for not taking better care of him.

The carriage started up again, this time a little faster. They crossed a small hump of a bridge and Charlotte wondered if the water underneath was a tributary to the Thames, she pondered on how many carriages must cross the bridge each day, and how often did the folk in these houses leave and return for the city? She realised she knew nothing of this neighbourhood, she might as well have been in a foreign country.

'What do they do,' she asked Mrs Johnson. 'All these people in these lovely houses?'

'All sorts, my dear. Some are gentry, some are politicians, traders, ship owners, shop owners.'

And yes, she could imagine it then. People had jobs and businesses; there were many new furniture shops, clothes shops, haberdashery shops, even tea-rooms. Nicholas had said the heyday of the fast ships might come to an end with the growing number of steam ships and trains but even if they did, all the trade and industry had changed things for the better, there was work if you looked for it, and there was every opportunity for new ventures.

'What do you do back home?' Mrs Johnson invaded her thoughts.

'What do you mean?'

'It's obvious you work for a living. Your hands are red and chapped.'

Charlotte drew her hands back.

'Don't worry. I won't tell the aunt.'

Charlotte was grateful for that at least.

The city spread across miles and miles of land, Charlotte could not comprehend the enormity of it.

'It's so small,' she said.

'What is?'

'Where we live in comparison to here. My mother lived in London for a while before.'

'Before what, dear?'

'Before me.'

And the moon made a sudden appearance and lit her frowning face for a few seconds.

The road was bumpy and the carriage rocked so they had to hold on. Charlotte was glad of the crunch of horses' hooves and carriage wheels as they trundled over a rough road. It meant they could be quiet and she gathered her thoughts, it might be that Mrs Johnson was spying for the aunt, trying to gather information about her to use against her later. Her friendliness could be a trap. Then Charlotte wondered when she had started being so mistrustful of people? Perhaps she always had been, perhaps she'd had to be to keep her family together.

'One of us ought to ride up top,' said Mrs Johnson. 'A better view to spot Will if he's out there somewhere.'

'I'll go,' said Charlotte.

Chapter Twelve

Sally turned around to look at her empty cottage in the dusk, then she walked briskly down the alley and slipped a note under May Fuller's back door, informing May of the journey she was about to undertake. She had written that she would make the journey by her own steam, and thought this comment would amuse May.

Sally could hear children's laughter from inside May's cottage as the woman's children were being bathed one by one in a tin bath by the fire. May would be holding out a towel to wrap each child in when they shivered out.

Sally sensed gargoyles sniggering above her as she cut across the church path.

'*Now then, Mrs Mayhew, where are you going in your fine black feathered hat? Hmm? Hmm? Raise the hem of your brown skirt or it will get wet!*'

Sally thought how the dead stay silent in the graveyard, so much leaning to listen to the whispers that the gravestones had begun to fall over.

'John, John,' she muttered. She kept her head down for twenty minutes or so until she reached the stable-yard where she knew a carriage was getting ready to take passengers to Wells to catch the night train to London.

The carriage seated four people, three were occupied, and because she had hoped to travel alone she climbed in with some hesitation casting a wary glance at the other passengers. There was a small red and blue rug on the vacant seat and she quickly took up the last woollen chequered offering and covered her lap, and then she wrapped her black shawl tightly around her.

'Good evening, I'm Doctor Farish, I'm returning to London after a short break in Cromer. The shipwreck will give me another story to tell when I get home.'

The doctor was aged about fifty, he was a little overweight, he had lost most of his hair but he appeared to make up for this loss with abundant greying curly sideburns, he was smartly dressed in a generous tweed suit. He had been hugging a holdall which he carefully placed under his carriage seat.

'Did you see the poor drowned man on the beach?' asked the other lady passenger. Sally thought her young with pretty defined features, she had sleek black hair tied up under a navy velvet hat and she wore a matching navy-blue travelling suit.

'Yes, unfortunately I got closer to him than I dare say. Cromer's doctor asked for a second opinion and he knew I was in town and asked me to confirm his initial examination.'

'But my husband is a doctor too, isn't that a coincidence?'

Dr Farish shook hands and the other man. Dr Pope, introduced himself, and asked his opinion of the incident on the beach.

Dr Farish looked at Sally. Sally was overcome with a need for laudanum, all these terrible things that happen …

'That's enough talk of things we can't change. Let's look ahead instead,' said Dr Farish.

He was kindly at least, and the lady who was obviously with her newish husband looked at Sally with curiosity for a moment and then looked down, she remained quiet for a few minutes until the coachman cracked his whip and the horses began pulling.

'When my husband and I ride out in a carriage we make sure the coachman has a small aneroid barometer which can be carried in a watch-pocket. I wonder if this coachman is aware of them, he might like to know whether or not to put on his mackintosh before he starts each journey? And did you know there's an excellent mackintosh been designed, it has false cuffs with an elastic band inside which …'

Sally found herself in a trance-like state and was sure it was caused by the woman's nervous chatter, she picked up some more talk of bicycle fiends that made the horses rear and then the woman switched back to talking randomly about Cromer's shops and walks, and even the food they'd eaten in the small hotel where they'd been staying.

'And you doctor, where did you stay?' Mrs Pope suddenly asked.

Doctor Farish told them his daughter had recently given birth and lived in Cromer. His wife had decided to stay on for a short time to help her adjust to the new arrival.

'And what pray, is your daughter doing living so far away from her parents?'

'Her husband is an architect; he has offices in the town. The coast here is up and coming for new builds and hotels, there's talk of bringing the railway to the town and area, which will bring many more visitors to the town. And of course, there's Norwich city 25 miles away, and all the places in-between.'

Sally mostly looked out of the carriage window after that. They were travelling along the coast road, at times she could see the horizon blurred into a dark grey image of sea and night sky. They passed two churches of the East and West Runtons, the lanterns and candles lights from inside the windows looked warm and welcoming.

Out at sea she saw lanterns wavering on a tall ship which seemed to sail parallel to them, then the road curved over a bridge and trotted past a Traveller's Inn, thankfully they didn't stop.

Soon the woman's husband had fallen asleep, his head rested against the side of the carriage, every now and then he made little snoring noises, his moustache twitched and he wriggled his nose, which made the other doctor look at Sally and wink. Sally smiled, it was unusual to find a man with such humour.

'We are approaching Sheringham,' said the doctor. 'Have you visited Sheringham, Mrs ...?'

'Mayhew,' answered Sally. 'Yes, a long time ago. They have, or had a very fine bookshop.'

'You like to read?'

'I used to before I lost my husband at sea,' she replied. And then the party fell into silence for the rest of the journey to Wells.

It was the smell of coal-smoke and steam that caused Sally to lift her eyes. She was taken by the beauty of the movement of steam and the hisses and grinding of yellow oil as it seeped between wheels. And the grand black engine that seemed to speak to her and invite her to enter the realms of the living –

Let me take you into my world of fast tracks, cocooned for a journey. Let me take you from the sea to the madhouse of the city. Let me show you vantage points. Come inside, leave your troubles behind you, it chuffed.

The ticket office was a small red brick building, unusual for North Norfolk, most buildings were made of flint and brick, perhaps new builds would buck the trend, wondered Sally. Inside, a young man in a black uniform sat at a desk behind black bars. His desk was illuminated by a double lamp, he twisted a rather pretty glass shade around so he could see her face better, on his side the lamp lit his face by a glaring large bulb, she could see the wick burning and she could smell kerosene, intense fumes filled the ticket office and the smell was stronger at the desk, it made her head swoon.

'How much is the last train to London?' she heard her small voice ask.

'Yew wanna ticket?'

She nodded.

'Single?'

She nodded again.

'Return?'

'One way. Third class, late night special, please.'

'Yew need to book three days in advance for a special.'

'But it's an emergency. I have to get to London.'

'Dew yew 'ave a bona-fida Angler's ticket? I can issue a ticket for three days from London return. Yew could travel in reverse. There's a special rate for Anglers.'

'How much is a normal third-class ticket?'

'Single?'

'Yes.'

'Ten shillings and sixpence.'

'What!?'

'Ten shillings and sixpence.'

'Third-class?'

'Yep. If you are a member of the bona-fida Anglers club I can give yew a ticket for five shillings and thruppence.'

'How much is it to join the Angler's club?'

'A shilling.'

'Do you know where I can get one?' She asked even though she knew she wouldn't have enough money to travel to London. Pretending to go for an Anglers club card would give her an excuse to slip away without embarrassment in front of the other travellers.

149

He wrote down an address, and handed it over. 'There's a couple of schooners sailing tonight, they'll take you for half-a-crown.'

'Really?'

'Aye.'

'Just for interest if I gave you three days' notice, how much then?'

'With special circumstances it's negoshible. It's decided above me. If yew write a letter I'll see it gets passed on with yewer request.'

'I'll have to think about it.'

'If yew come back in the morning yew could 'ave a special day return and not use the return tomorrow night.'

'What?'

'Aye. Four shillings, first-class, three-second, and two shillings third-class.'

'Do I need to book in advance?'

'No. Yew just turn up and ask for the day return to the exhibition in London.'

'All right then.'

'But if yew want to go tonight yew'd best go by boat.'

'I'll wait until morning. I'll take a third class ticket for the special day return for tomorrow, in advance if you don't mind.'

'Wait!' Doctor Farish was fidgeting in the queue behind her. 'My wife should have been travelling with me. You could travel on her ticket.'

'Well,' said the ticket officer,' 'It's unusual,' he stroked his chin.

'Who's to know,' asked the doctor. He handed his tickets over to be checked by the ticket officer, and then he handed the tickets back to Doctor Farish and peered behind to the door as if he thought someone might jump in and catch him breaking the rules. They waited for the recently married couple to get their tickets checked and the little party made their way through a small entry gate onto the platform. Un-protesting, Sally climbed aboard a dark purple carriage, steam hissed and wound through the undercarriages.

Once, when John had come home early in the December mist, Sally had been standing in the living room (she couldn't remember why), he'd walked over to the fireplace wearing a gansey, she had said, 'Let me mend the thread before it runs.' As he pulled the jumper over his head she had noticed how strong and hard his arm muscles were, how the hairs on his arms were still blonde from the summer sun, she noticed how his black hair was still thick and in need of a trim. She'd put her fingers in his hair and instead of taking the gansey from him, she had let it drop to the floor. Then she remembered the hardness of his back, the way he turned around taking off his blue cotton short sleeved shirt. She'd put her arms around him feeling his chest and his belly with circles as though it was the first time. He had turned towards her, shaking, and she heard the softness of the fire as a layer of red hot ashes fell to another level. How she'd tilted her head to look up to him. How he'd taken a sharp breath. How something changed between them, a realization that no matter what, they'd always have this to remember, that sense of being where you belong – like coming home. She had not been second-best on that occasion.

Sally was jolted by a sliding of levers underneath the carriage, perhaps the train had changed track. They were being pulled towards night, parallel to the dark outside world along iron rails that no man might dig underneath for centuries to come.

Dr Farish was asleep or feigning sleep, the couple were asleep or dozing. How odd that the four of them had slipped into this companionship so soon after meeting. A trust had developed between them and she wondered if it would just be for the journey. She thought they must have misjudged her, she was not the person she used to be, she was paper thin, white paper, black holes for eyes. Earlier, when she'd shivered, the doctor explained how the steam (or water?) travelled down pipes in the carriage and heated them once they got moving, and she'd looked away to the window and seen her reflection which answered back, 'Do I look like I care?' and she was ashamed of herself for not being more interested and attentive. Wisps of what reflected back like white hair had escaped from her black hat, oil lamps swayed as the train set off, and then the doctor offered his green woollen rug, and she'd wanted to pull it up over her head and disappear from these people, from the train but she had no choice other than to smile and say, 'No thank you.'

Keep trundling on, as her neighbour, May, would say.

While she dozed she noted Dr Farish every so often producing a silver pocket watch from the chest pocket of his tweed jacket, he would flick the lid and hold the watch face up to the lamplight. She became mesmerised by the rocking movement of the lamp, the repetitive sounds of the carriage on the tracks and the following carriage and the one after that … passing time, moving on, she was taking control, changing things for Charlotte and to bring Will home where he belonged.

Oh yes, thought Henry, seeing the whip of the lad disappearing through a dark hedgerow. Wherever Will had been going, and whatever he had intended to do, Henry sensed Will had changed direction and wasn't going to do it now. Will was shifting like a ghost in the night. Before he'd been slow and directional sticking to paths and walkways, now he was shifting like a hunted fox. Was Will in on Charlotte's plan? Was Will sneaking around in the middle of the night to do negotiations for more gold sovereigns? He hadn't set out to follow Will, this outing was unexpected. How clever the lad was to spot 'im and know 'im and run from 'im.

He could go back and break into the house whose address he had repeated to 'imself back in Cromer going up and down the jetty thinking what a grand name Summerville House was. He could go back and break in like he had intended to do and question the girl to find out her story. His guess was that John, the father (there he'd said his name in his head and nothing awful had happened) had stashed more sovereigns somewhere and the girl had found them. How long ago had she found them? The worst thing was the girl hadn't shared them wi' Sally. Poor deluded Sally who had cared for them bairns (well, tried her best too) all these years and there was 'im, chipping in, oh yes he had, and how had they repaid 'im? By running off and selling ill begotten sovereigns and maybe other items of gold what could make a difference to their lives now, that's how.

The lad had a way about 'im, as if the fog creeped behind him slithering in obeyance to 'im. Aye, even a phantom horse appeared from nowhere and whinnied to carry 'im off to the stars, yet the lad declined the offer. And then a fox barked, a dog fox that stank of filth and hung his head wi' shame at being a night thief. And the lad had looked up at chimneys, here and there streaks of smoke puffed grey into grey, and Henry had twiddled wi' the six boxes of matches he'd brought from the little match girl in the market. The girl in the pitifully thin dress that shouldn't be allowed anymore, and when he'd questioned her, she'd replied, 'I'm twelve! I can do what I want,' with such fierce indignation that he paid her double what she asked, and then she'd smiled and winked and he knew he'd been had. What was the world coming too when a little snippet of a girl could get away wi' that?

Henry sidled up to the hedgerow and when he looked down he saw a dead blackbird, he picked it up by a stiff leg and examined it and he thought it's neck was broke and someone must have chucked it there but when he looked closer he saw blood in its belly and realised it had been shot. Who would shoot a blackbird? He put it back and covered it with damp leaves. The world was full of mysterious people wi' dark thoughts. But he wondered if it was a sign to follow the lad or go back to the house? What if the lad was about to fall foul to some negotiator? He could save the lad and then the lad would share his secrets.

Looking at the dead blackbird had cost Henry a vital minute. He figured Will was heading for the docks vicinity; the lad would get his trading done for the stash and then head for the safety of Captain O'Rourke's vessel.

Will was startled for a moment by the unexpectedness of coming across a church even though it was on his map, its windows glowered with flickering yellow candle light. Will was struck by a thought that told him he was ungrateful, childish even. He could retrace the long way back to Summerville House. He was old enough to know it was a house of safety and what he was doing was the act of a child.

He heard a small cry, like that of a muffled herring gull. He looked around, there were some gravestones leaning haphazardly, the wall around the church was low and much of the wrought iron railings were missing. He climbed through a gap onto a hardened path that glittered with frosty patches. He stood in the light wind and listened for the sound again.

Charlotte had discussed the word 'faith' with him. She'd explained the difference between faith and belief. He'd like to have faith, something to hold on to, and he considered that this moment was something that could give him faith, this quiet church glowing in the night with trellised ivy climbing up the grand archway and ancient door.

Then he heard the cry again. This time it sounded like someone saturated with grief, perhaps asleep behind a gravestone, perishing in the night. He shivered. A stone angel watched him, she stared, holding dead still. He listened for footfall, or something gliding, a knot forming in his stomach. He believed in the afterlife, ghosts and spirits. Sometimes his father's shadow back home watched over him when he ran the beach at night. His father left signs, a piece of pottery, a mermaid's purse, broken shells, or more recently Captain O'Rourke when he was overboard, he brought the man to the right place at the right time.

But here he was now with a stone angel.

'Who-a-you?'

Will couldn't run. His feet were glued to the spot. He took a deep breath and steadied himself. Speed was his strength if only he could find it.

'We're locked out.' A young boy's voice called out.

'Locked out?' Will asked.

'Aye. Locked out.'

'Show yourself,' said Will, somewhat relieved to hear a boy's voice.

'Can't remember when I was seen, proper-like clean, like you and stuff.'

'It's freezing 'ain't it?' said Will coaxingly.

'Aye, it could freeze yer wotsits off,' came the reply. A boy crept from the ground behind a gravestone and unfolded himself. If Will hadn't heard the boy speak he might have thought him coming right up from inside the grave. His hair was the first thing you noticed about him. Will's eyes were drawn to it, the boy's hair was shoulder length and black, it stuck out in all directions, yet it was stiff and in sections like it had been set with something, the boy peered out through gaps in his fringe, tears streaked down his filthy face. The boy was lanky and so very thin his wrists and hands looked odd sticking out from the mud-coated jacket he shivered in. He had a grey muffler around his neck and he pulled it up over his mouth now. Will noticed his trousers were rolled up at the bottom and it wasn't until the boy came closer that he realised the boy was barefooted and the reason he looked like he wore shoes was because his feet and ankles were encrusted with mud.

'Set in stone these,' the boy tried to wriggle his toes. 'What's yer name?'

'Will.' He held out his hand.

The boy took it and laughed.

157

'Ain't you proper? Took me an hour to walk 'ere from the docks it did. But the vicar always ses, 'Get 'ere after eleven and yer sleep wi' the dead!''

'So he's in there?'

'Aye. The bastard's in the back wi' the little uns. Can't blame 'im. As we get older we're more likely to go off, so he bolts the doors and locks the wee ones in. My fault.

'Ain't seen you before?'

'I'm not from round here.'

'Yer in trouble?'

'Aye. I think I might be.'

'Well I'm bloody freezin'.'

'An hour's walk to the docks you said?' Will queried.

'Yes.'

'I know where we can get a bed, food too,' said Will. 'Can you get us there?' Will could see the 'Merganser' in his head, soup and bread, swinging in a hammock – and a tub of hot water for this boy.

'We 'ave to go through gardens and climb fences for short cuts like.'

'I can do that. Wait.' From his pocket he took out wrapped bread and cheese he'd made in kitchen at Summerville House. 'For emergencies,' he said.

'Better than holy soup,' the boy grinned.

'What's your name?'

'The Artful Dodger.'

'No really?'

'Oliver.'

'Come on.'

'All right, it's Peter.'

'Okay, Peter, lead the way.'

'I'm lucky' Peter said, looking down. 'A hot potato and bread n cheese all in a day!'

Henry thought how some people were un-subconsciously aware when a stranger passed by their property at night. He noticed a lamp would flicker on and waver by a window, sometimes a door would open. Animals were so much more sensitive, dogs would bark, cats would meow loudly and pelt out from a hidey-hole, then they would sit at the end of a drive and look from left to right as if to say, '*I know you're there.*'

When Will had left the churchyard with an accomplice Henry was 'knocked for six' because it became real then, that Will was in on whatever the girl was up too. How could she send the lad out this time of the night to do her dirty work? She had turned hard and cruel that one.

Henry wanted to be haunted by memories of where he was but he had no idea of this locality, this was a strange part of London to him, many of the houses had been built since he was a lad. The houses went from grand individual places like Summerville House, to more modest town houses. He wondered who lived in all of these houses. There must be loads of maids and servants. At strategic points there were stable-yards with paddocks. The paddocks were in darkness, there was a different silence about them, silhouettes of winter trees lined the boundaries, and some had land that banked up or down, patterns of mist and shadows abstracted make-belief people. Some horses were out in the field, some stabled up against the cold. More often than not several carriages were lined up outside the stables.

A swampy path frosted over and glittered as the night moved on another hour.

Not long after Sally had lost her husband, Henry had been looking in on the family and had been shocked to find Sally in a trance-like state. The girl was hovering over Sally as her mother sat staring into space in a chair. Henry had picked Sally up and carried through to the couch in the parlour (how light she had been?) and he'd put a cover over her and said, 'Fetch the doctor,' to Charlotte.

'I did, and this is the consequence. Has she overdosed?' she'd replied, Then she'd bit her bottom lip as if to say, *Is this my fault?*

Then he saw the lad who was about four then, he picked him up and took him upstairs to bed so he could come back down and ponder over what to do about Sally for a bit. When he got the lad upstairs and put 'im in his cot the lad had said, 'Turn on the dark, Henry.' This had blown Henry away at the time, he often told the story as if the lad were his own. He hadn't said, 'Blow out the lamp, Henry,' no he hadn't. The lad had a whole way of thinking all of his own.

Henry had stayed the night, making sure Sally was on her side. The girl never slept, she curled beside her mother on a chair and stared ahead and thought, God knows what, until she'd get up to put some coal on the fire or check on Will.

Perhaps he'd neglected the kids of late. Perhaps he'd got too involved wi' the kegs of brandy. Perhaps you were supposed to do more and take more of an interest and be more kindly so the kids trusted you, not feared you. Perhaps you weren't supposed to follow them and chase them through churchyards and make death threats.

He stopped for a moment to breathe in the cold damp air.

'Will, lad!' he shouted.

It was spontaneous. It woke some of the neighbourhood. It made Will and his accomplice run for their lives.

'No, lad, no,' he mumbled, rubbing his eyes.

'Yer stopping 'ere?' asked the coachman in a deep gruff voice.

'Yes,' answered Charlotte. They were the first words the coachman had spoken in what seemed like an hour since they'd stopped the coach and explained Charlotte would ride 'up top' to see if she could spot Will from the vantage point.

The coachman had never said a word in reply, he'd just handed Charlotte a neatly folded blanket which she'd gratefully wrapped around her head and shoulders, she'd been please to find it big enough to wrap around her body too. She'd tried not to think who else the blanket might have been wrapped around, then began to notice it smelled a little horsey, and it was too dark to see if it was stained or covered in hair. She worried about getting horse hair on her new clothes but it was so cold sitting there that she was soon grateful for its meagre warmth.

'I hope you find the lad,' the coachman nodded from under his great tall hat and upturned collar.

'Thank you.' So he had been looking out after all. 'Apart from the docks, this is the only place he might come.'

'You related?'

He meant Mrs Johnson inside the coach, or maybe Aunt Mary. 'Not really. We know the girl, Alice Merryweather, she befriended us when …' Charlotte was already saying too much and stopped saying anymore.

'Oh, she's good at befriending, that one.'

'You know her?'

'I know her coachman.'

Yes, she supposed they might know each other, raising tall hats in passing, scrunched down under mackintoshes in the cold blustery winds.

The coachman jumped down and came around her side to help her and then opened the carriage door for Mrs Johnson.

In her imagination, Charlotte had conjured up a palace for Alice to live in. In fact the Merryweather's residence was actually a modest town house, with adjoining neighbours on both sides. There were so many houses in the cul-de-sac she couldn't count them and the maze of houses looked pretty much the same in the dark.

There was no sign of Will. If he was here surely there would be some activity such as lanterns lighting up the house through the windows. Alice's house, number 77, like the rest, was in darkness.

The coachman surprised her by running up several white steps and knocking loudly on the door.

Mrs Johnson took the shawl from her head and neck and arranged it around her shoulders, Charlotte hurried up the steps after her.

Minutes later, Charlotte was standing in a cold hallway, dimly lit by a manservant holding a solitary candle, he had dressed hurriedly and had donned a grey blanket around his shoulders. Thankfully he recognised Mrs Johnson and the conversation moved quickly as she enquired about Will.

The man lit several candles in a silver candelabra on a sideboard; the light illuminated what Charlotte could now see was an impressive hallway.

On the floor, either side of an imposing grandfather clock stood two medium-sized carved wooden elephants, the wall in front of her had a framed, snarling tiger's head, below it a large birdcage hung from a stand, the cage was covered over with a dark velvet cover, a squawk was building up from inside the cage. The staircase leading off the hallway had wide steps and mahogany banisters with huge carved posts, there were archways, and walls with various sized antlers, a maze of multi-coloured tiles beneath her feet, and on the sideboard a silver bowl with at least a dozen oranges in it.

It was three-quarters past midnight. It was her birthday, she was a year older, seventeen in fact. Will was missing, her father was long dead, and her mother was miles away, she was in a stranger's house in a strange city with a strange woman about to come face to face with a girl she hardly knew.

Tiredness swept over her, she had to sit in one of two chairs just inside the hallway, it was sprung and covered in a dark red velvet, it had heavily carved arms which spiralled outwards and she thought they would curl in around her and hold her tight.

Mrs Johnson sat next to her. Charlotte fought back tears. Mrs Johnson's warm hand was thrust on her cold one as tears streaked down her cheeks. Charlotte swallowed trying to stop the flow of tears, she was suddenly leaning forward and covering her face with her hands.

'Just don't tell her about your relationship with Nicholas,' whispered Mrs Johnson. 'At least not yet. Not until we've found Will.'

'But—'

'I'll think of some other reason to tell her why you're staying with us.'

'I can't lie to this girl. Why should I?'

'You must.'

Charlotte heard voices on the stairs and a pattering of feet. Alice, wrapped in a fine white wool shawl glided towards them, her white nightgown trailing on a richly coloured Indian stair carpet.

'Mrs Johnson? Charlotte?' she cried in a concerned voice.

Alice seemed smaller, more fragile than Charlotte remembered.

'What on earth—'

'It's Will,' Charlotte blurted out. 'He's took off. We thought he might have come here?'

'Will? He's not here. No one's here. Why would he come here?'

'Your card. He has your card with your address on it. You made an impression on him.'

Alice sighed and made a little, 'Ah,' sound as if Will wasn't the first boy to have a crush on her. For some reason Charlotte found she was annoyed by this.

'Come in. Come through to the parlour.'

Alice ushered them. The manservant who had somehow managed to disappear and reappear in dark trousers and a black sweater, walked through an archway and opened a door for them. A few orange embers in a fireplace gave an eerie glow to the room. The manservant went straight over and placed two logs on the fire; flames quickly sparked and crackled.

Alice took the candle he had placed on the mantelpiece and lit various candles around the room.

Charlotte wondered where the other servants were. Shouldn't they be bustling around?

'Your parents?' asked Mrs Johnson.

'At our country house for Christmas, with the other servants – except for old Minnie, and she's as deaf as a doorpost you know. I wouldn't wake her.'

Charlotte noticed a frown cover Mrs Johnson's face as she looked from Alice to the manservant, it was only then that Charlotte realised he was Alice's coachman, he'd been driving her the day Alice befriended them.

'They left you here alone with him?' said Mrs Johnson, rather rudely Charlotte thought.

'Why wouldn't they,' answered Alice. 'I'm twenty-years old, not twelve. I can be trusted to look after the house.'

Charlotte would never have dared to speak to Mrs Johnson like that. She was beginning to warm to Alice again, perhaps because of her frankness and confidence.

Alice turned to Charlotte and said, 'Anyway, what's happened to Will? Why has he run off? Is that man chasing him again?'

'What man,' Mrs Johnson queried.

'The man that was chasing them in the market, he looked mighty fierce.'

'He was just a pickpocket – a thief – he tried to rob us of what little we had.' Charlotte lied, and she glared at Alice with a pleading look.

'Ah yes, we outwitted him,' Alice played along.

'Coincidences are a funny thing aren't they,' Mrs Johnson said. 'Like fate throwing you two together,' she said with an expression of a know-all.

'Please, sit,' said Alice.

166

Charlotte sat in a plump armchair, her hands resting briefly on luscious velvet arms, dark blue orchid-type flowers wove amongst a cream background and here and there velvet green birds dipped into red tendrils. She moved her hands and rested them on her knee like her mother had taught her years ago.

She noticed a large gilt mirror over the fireplace and the coachman was standing staring into it, watching them through their reflections.

'John,' said Alice. 'John, please get Mrs Johnson and Charlotte a brandy.'

'No. Not for me,' said Charlotte.

'A sherry then?'

'No. A glass of water please.'

John, the coachman, quietly left the room.

Mrs Johnson sat on a settee of the same pattern as the armchair, Alice stood by the fireplace now. In the centre of the room was a large deep square glass topped table, under the glass were carved jungle animals. Charlotte found she was gazing at the animals.

'My father's,' said Alice. 'From India.'

'It's beautiful. Will would love it.'

'What are we going to do about Will,' said Alice, as if she were part of this, as if it were her problem and not just Charlotte's.

'If he didn't come here where else would he go?' Who else does he know?' asked Alice. And then as if the thought had only just occurred to her, she asked, 'How do you know Mrs Johnson? Why is she with you?'

There was a moment's pause then Mrs Johnson said, 'She's a friend of the family. Well her father was. More of an acquaintance of your father's that Mr O'Rourke kept communications open with.'

'Open with? What does that mean?'

'It was a long time ago. Like I said, it had more to do with your father than Nicholas's father. But the two were good friends and isn't it funny how coincidences bring people back together. Have you heard the story of how your father was in a shipwreck when you were very little?'

Alice pondered for a moment. 'James, my elder brother mentioned it once, in a fabricated story, I thought.'

'It wasn't fabricated, my dear. Charlotte's father risked his life to save your father's life.'

Alice stared at Charlotte like her attraction to her was just as Mrs Johnson said, fate.

Charlotte was flabbergasted, her arms tensed and she shivered. What was Mrs Johnson saying! She stared back at Alice.

'Yes,' continued Mrs Johnson. 'Nicholas stays ashore sometimes at their lodging house in Cromer. And when Charlotte said she had business in London, he invited them to stay at Summerville House because of the connections between the families.'

Mrs Johnson was adding to the lies? thought Charlotte. What was she saying these things for? Nicholas had only stayed at their cottage once hadn't he? Or had she not noticed him before. She would check her books when she got home.

'So we would have met – eventually,' Alice said, delighted. 'How wonderful. How absolutely wonderful. How exciting.' Alice stood up and moved around the room clapping her hands.

Charlotte was speechless. Her mother's telling of the story about the rescue had been so long ago, but it was true, her father had saved a man's life and had been rewarded for the deed.

John, the coachman, came back into the room with a tray and of drinks.

Mrs Johnson took her brandy and downed it in one swallow. 'I should like to stay here if possible in case Will decides to come after all. Would you allow your coachman to take Charlotte to the docks, see if he's made his way to the safety of the captain's vessel?'

'What a plan! It is a plan isn't it?' exclaimed Alice. She came over to Charlotte and pulled her up by her hands. 'Of course I'll go with you.'

Charlotte was taken aback. She desperately needed this girl's help to find Will. Perhaps she would let Mrs Johnson's exaggerated half-truths rest. If Alice's Merryweather's father really had been saved by her father then it would be right to accept Alice's help.

'Shall I go and prepare the coach?' asked John.

'We shall find some very warm clothes!' was Alice's reply.

'Mrs Johnson, is it true? Is Alice's father really the man my father rescued? I can hardly believe it,' said Charlotte. 'I remember a little of the story.'

169

Alone with Mrs Johnson, she stood up and walked around the room.

'Alice's mother,' replied the stout woman, wrapping her black shawl around her and clinging to it so tight her knuckles were white. 'Alice's mother …' she paused, staring at the painting on the wall.

'Yes, what is it?' Charlotte moved over and stood in front of a portrait Mrs Johnson was staring at; the woman in the painting was adorned in a black riding suit, she leaned on a black stallion, she wore a black hat with two black feathers in it, parts of her hair were visible, and it was jet black, quite unlike Alice's hair.

'Alice takes after her father?'

The woman in the painting seemed quite tall, taller than Alice that much Charlotte could tell. As she gazed into the woman in the portraits eyes her heart starting beating rapidly, she took a sharp intake of breath, then her eyes moved to the jewellery the woman in the portrait wore around her neck. The room began to spin.

Mrs Johnson put a hand out to steady her. Had Mrs Johnson seen the pearls she wore around her neck! She was sure she had kept them hidden.

'Sit down, Charlotte, you're so very tired.'

And Charlotte did so, sinking into the armchair.

'Alice doesn't much look like her mother does she?'

'Alice takes after her father then,' Charlotte repeated, blotting out any similarities between Alice's mother and herself, the hair, the eyes …

Alice burst into the room with a swish of dark blue velvets before they could say anymore. 'I have blankets for us, Charlotte, dear.'

Charlotte had to find Will but she had never meant to involve Alice. Now she wondered if her mother or her father *had* stolen the jewels. Could her father have rescued Alice's father and then gone to their house to claim the reward, thieving from the family, and they hadn't reported him because they owed him Alice's father's life?

She recalled the moment she acquired the jewels. There had been a violent row between her parents, her mother had been shouting and running up the clifftop. Charlotte had taken Will out of the way and she had sat him on the sand on the beach when the jewels came hurtling over the cliffs and had fallen glittering and splashing in the sea. Some more shouting from above followed. Charlotte, couldn't resist, she'd waded in the water and retrieved what she could find and took the jewels home wrapped up in the baby's shawl.

She never heard her parents mention the jewels again; she never told her mother she had them. She tried to think if there had been any relief of tension at home because of them but if anything, the tension had been worse, her father silent, and her mother angry, nothing ever seemed to be resolved between them after the incident.

And now, here was Alice, brimming with kindness, about to help her find Will. She would throttle Will for putting her in this situation when she found him.

171

Henry chased the lads for what seemed like a good hour to him. He'd catch a glimpse of them up a path and they'd run around the back of some house, climb through another hedge and then disappear again. A lesser man would have given up but Henry never gave up a chase unless he was well and truly beat, and these scrawny lads would not get the better of him. He could tell that Will's accomplice was not a man by the way he scrambled and occasionally shrieked like a mad fox, a man would never shriek in a chase, especially when it woke half the neighbourhood. They weren't good at hiding their tracks either, leaving gaping hedges and snapping twigs, let alone all the cats and dogs making a racket.

Some of the streets had new gas lamps hereabouts and he knew they were approaching the docks.

Henry doubted their real accomplice was waiting at the docks, the man they'd be selling the gold sovereigns too. They knew they were being followed and they wouldn't lead Henry to this man, nay, they'd be heading for the safety of the naive captain and his crew.

The lads stopped running for a few seconds, he could see their silhouettes in the distance, they were shaking hands and then Will took off as if he was running for his life again.

Henry went in pursuit, he could hear his oilskin coat rattling and the rubbery clump of his boots on the slippy road. He was closing in. Good job too.

They were at a part of the dockside no longer recognisable to him. New gas lampposts had been erected by a new wall, he was running past great snarling dolphins that looked more like serpents curled around metal posts, under the lamplight they had eyes and tongues that flickered red and yellow. The black water slopped against groynes and yet there were no boats here, a sign of times to come or what? And the lad was in catching distance. The lad stooped over. Will had had a rotten cough for so long.

'Lad, lad, I ain't gonna hurt yer,' he shouted.

And Will was proper doubled over and coughing. He caught up.

'Now I gotcha!' he held on to the scruff of a tweedy jacket. He pulled off the lad's new cap.

'You!'

'Gotcha, mister.'

'Filthy bloody mudlark. Where's Will?'

'He'll be on the boat now, mister.'

'I oughter ring yer bloody neck.' He let go of Peter in disgust. 'After I fed you and all?'

'I didn't know it was you, mister.'

'No, I don't suppose you did. Got a new jacket and cap out of it though, eh?'

'Aye that I did, mister.'

'He'll be on the boat then?'

'If you say so.'

'Get on your way, before I change me mind and do for you in the river.'

Henry's disappointment sank right down to his feet. The world was often black or bleak, he thought. This boy, this mudlark, whom he'd fed and would have fed again and again if he saw him regularly, had played a trick on him. And what about Will? Had it been his idea? He should have known this boy wasn't Will; Will wasn't nearly as tall as this boy, nor anywhere near as filthy. This boy had bare feet too – wasn't the world supposed to be changing?

'Let go of me then, matey!' shouted the boy.

Henry had moved his arm around the boy's neck and was applying pressure. The boy was really scrawny; he could feel the boy's ribs with his other arm. The boy squirmed.

'Yer as thin as a sparrow.'

'Yer said I could go?' the boy gasped.

'LET GO OF HIM, HENRY!'

Will appeared, he stood yards away and removed a filthy muffler from around his head and exposed his shock of blonde hair. Henry looked from one boy to the other still disbelieving he was fooled so easily.

'Will. Lad.'

'LET GO OF PETER.'

Henry released his grip and pushed Peter to the ground. Peter curled up as though Henry would kick him.

'I've not hurt 'im.'

'Looks like you have to me.'

174

'He's all right.'

'You all right, Peter?'

Peter nodded. 'Thought you'd gone. Run now, Will!'

'What do you want of me, Henry?' asked Will, ignoring Peter.

'To explain myself, Will. I only ever wanted to explain.'

'Explain what?'

'That night. On the beach. I never laid a finger on Claude.'

'Claude?

'The Frenchie on the beach. '*Respirer, Claude. Respirer!*'' shouted Henry.

'What?'

'It was me, Will. I was shouting on the beach. *Breathe, Claude, Breathe*! And his arms, see. Like this.' Henry put his arms out in the air and moved them like bellows in and out. 'I was trying to get the water out of the Frenchie's lungs.'

'But I saw you put your hand over his mouth.'

'Nay, lad. I was opening his mouth. It were full of seaweed. I was doing sweeps see, like this.' Henry demonstrated with his fingers curving around. 'I couldn't get 'im to breathe again, so I took back the money I'd given 'im earlier for the kegs. We only had part of the delivery anyway so I was entitled to it. You know about what I do right? It pays for things. It keeps us going.'

'Come here, Peter,' said Will.

The boy on the ground crawled very quickly on his hands and knees towards Will.

175

'I'm proud of yer, Will. I am. But you've got me all wrong.' Henry ran his hands through his hair and scratched his brown curly sideburns.

Will wasn't sure if Henry was lying or not. There was something earnest about Henry, some parts of his story rang true but the way he moved his lips suspiciously as if he was waiting for Will to make a decision and then pounce on him.

'But why would you chase me like that? You were going to murder me.'

'No, lad. It's the smuggling yer see. I couldn't let you tell anyone. I just wanted to scare you a bit.'

'Henry, I wouldn't have told.'

'I know that now, Will. I know. We were all het up.'

Will helped Peter up from the ground. Standing next to Peter he was doubly confident, doubly strong.

'Help's coming,' said Peter.

Will saw Henry's eyes flicker into the distance behind him.

'You summoned Captain O'Rourke?'

'No. I think all the shouting did that.'

'His boat's miles away down there.'

'We're just lucky then.'

'Aye, or something or someone is looking out for you.' Henry hesitated and said, 'That sister of yours. 'What's her business here?'

'Charlotte?' Will wasn't quite sure how to answer. He still didn't know if Henry was involved with Charlotte's jewels or if they were smuggled or stolen. What if she was betraying Henry? What if she'd stolen from him?'

'She's going to marry the captain, Nicholas O'Rourke,' he said, deciding not to mention the jewels at all.

'What?'

Henry was already in retreat, walking backwards as the captain and another man began to run towards him.

So Alice was made up in blue velvets and covered with a soft green lambs-wool blanket. The only flesh visible of her was her pale face, lit by the occasional glimpse of moonlight as it flooded through the windows of the carriage. Alice smiled at Charlotte, which was quite disarming even to Charlotte, thinking how that this girl had rescued her for the second time.

The coachman, Humphrey or John, had seemed dazed and somewhat on the point of protesting at going out at this hour but on scrutiny Charlotte suspected it was more for Alice's safety than his own discomfort.

'The docks can be a terrible place at night,' he'd said. 'Thieves, beggars and worse.'

'We'll be inside the carriage at all times, and besides we have you to protect us,' Alice had replied firmly.

John had answered, 'Yes. And if anything happens to you, your parents will hold me responsible.'

'Just do as I ask, John.'

177

What an odd lingering look had passed between them, thought Charlotte, for a manservant he seemed overly familiar.

Charlotte was once again struck with guilt as the carriage jolted forward. She'd acquired a quickened heartbeat with a rewinding of conversations between herself and Nicholas, and while she thought of him, her hands shook. She carried her silence with her secrets. She pondered on the jewels she had left behind (thank goodness) wrapped up and hidden at Summerville House. She wondered if her mother had carried a guilty secret when she had tossed the jewels into the sea. How her mother's anguish had been carried by the rushing wind down the cliffs where she had been standing. How loud her mother's sobbing had been. How *painful* her cries had sounded. And she imagined her mother had fallen into the soft ground and sobbed for hours with no one to find her, unaware her daughter looked after her baby son far below her, listening to her, and wading into the dark sea to retrieve the very things she had meant to get rid of. Perhaps the jewels were cursed what with all that happened afterwards. Her father drowning. Her mother's addiction.

If she hadn't been intent on selling the jewels she wouldn't be here now but then again, if she hadn't come to London Will might have drowned.

'Don't look so worried,' said Alice, interrupting her thoughts. 'We'll find Will.' And she reached across from under her blanket to touch Charlotte's bare hand with her gloved one. 'You're so cold.

Here, wrap underneath the blanket like me.' And she demonstrated making a stupid puppet under her blanket, its green mouth opening and closing like a snapping dragon.

Charlotte swallowed and turned to look into the street.

'Have you ever tried mint tea, or lemon tea?' asked Alice.

Charlotte shook her head.

'We have milk delivered in glass bottles here now. Do you have bottled milk where you come from?'

Charlotte couldn't help chuckling.

'Have you ever been to our part of the country, Alice?'

'No. Father has always refused to let us go. Though mother protests. She has asked him a million times, it's like an obsession with her. She dare not disobey him. We visit Brighton a couple of times a year. Father won't let us travel overseas. I should like to go to Europe, France and Spain. I've heard so much about them I feel as if I've been.'

No doubt she heard about these places through Nicholas, thought Charlotte. Just how friendly were they?

'Perhaps you will go one day, after the war between France and Germany is over.' she replied.

'Yes, perhaps I shall. I hope the war is over soon.'

'You are a wonderful artist,' stated Charlotte. 'I imagine the drawings you'd bring back from Europe would be amazing.'

'What makes you say that, dear Charlotte?'

'I … I've seen the illustrations by you in a book, they are quite exquisite.'

'Ah, the book. The little drawings in Nicholas' book?'

'Yes, quite.'

'I needed the money. Nicholas was kind enough to suggest me. The publishers were adamant that no one found out I was a woman. It just wouldn't do would it? A woman doing illustrations in a man's book.'

'What I don't understand is why he didn't do them himself. He's such a talented artist.'

'The difference is in the technical detail. Nicholas is all about lines and measurements, accuracies and detail. My crude sketches are about the emotion in the subject. That's why we complement each other you see? But you're right, really, he was doing me a favour, I really needed the money.'

'Why on earth would you need money? Don't you have an allowance or something?' The words slipped out of Charlotte's mouth quite sharply but she could not see any reason why someone of Alice's stature could possibly want for anything financially.

'My dear, a woman of her own means can do anything she wants, not be controlled – no – be expected to do whatever her parents demand of her.'

'But you're here, now. I don't see them controlling you. You seem like a free spirit.'

'It's a delusion. A brief reprieve. My parents would be horrified if they could see me now. They'd probably have me locked up in an asylum.' Alice sighed. 'I don't know, maybe I exaggerate.'

'You're lucky you have parents that care,' said Charlotte.

'Lucky? Is that what you call it?'

'You should be grateful.'

'Ha!'

'My father's dead.'

'Dead?'

'Yes. He went missing at sea several years ago.'

'I'm sorry, Charlotte. I just assumed he was still around,' Alice spoke sincerely.

'It's all right.'

'Your mother?'

'Took his loss badly. She hasn't been right since. The doctor put her on laudanum and it became a terrible habit. It's like I take care of Will. Like he's my responsibility.'

'And now you've gone and lost him. Don't worry we'll find him.'

Alice didn't pat her hand this time thankfully. They travelled for several miles in silence. Alice looked pensive, and Charlotte scanned the streets, until Alice suddenly broke in,

'How did you manage financially? Did your mother remarry?'

'Mother never worked again or remarried. It was down to me. We had a little given to us – from the poor law. But we would have starved on what they gave us. I managed to find work which pays the bills. Sometimes I take in guests, I oust Will from his bed into mine. Will also contributes by catching crabs and fish, and then there's the coal running which gives us fuel in the winter, and he gets paid a little from his job. And then there's also the contributions from Henry.'

'Who's Henry?'

'It's complicated. Henry appeared after father was lost at sea. Henry brings us food just about every week, a box of vegetables one week, bread and cheese the next, he keeps a constant supply of tea, some coal, and logs and other contraband.'

'Is he related to you?'

'Not yet. Rumour has it he is going to be our stepfather.'

'You sound like you don't approve?'

'Henry was the man chasing us in the market. It was him we were running from.'

'Oh how awful. Is he terribly bad?'

'He wasn't until recently.'

'Will seemed terrified of him. Does he beat you both?'

'It's odd isn't it; he's never laid a finger on us. Not yet anyway.'

'But he has the potential too? A reason in his head. And it's growing and growing as if it's about to burst.'

'You are funny, Alice, but yes, something like that.'

'Look out of the window.'

They were in a different part of the city, men had begun to appear wandering aimlessly, and some men leaned on posts smoking pipes or cigarettes.

'What are they doing?' asked Charlotte.

'I don't know. Waiting for a lady of the night, maybe, summing up courage to do some robbing, or maybe just hesitating before they go home to a crowded room with a wife and six children. But they have the potential to be threatening don't they? We women are portrayed as the weaker sex whatever, wherever we come from. I admire you greatly, Charlotte. You've kept your family together; you must have worked so hard.'

'You've no idea, but I'm no hero, Alice. It just happened. I've been lucky and unlucky. And to be honest I'm not sure we could have got through it all without Henry. I guess we owe him, perhaps if I'd talked to him—'

'Oh my goodness! Look! It's Will. He's with Nicholas and Tom!'

Sally took Dr Farish's arm as she stepped down from the train carriage in the early hours into a gust of cold air. She inhaled coal steam mixed with engine oil to the sound of the great black steam engine still hissing and winding down. Station guards stood down the line holding lanterns where dazed-looking passengers climbed down. Here and there a lantern light would disappear as a guard would step up into the carriage to retrieve someone's luggage. This wasn't necessary with their small group, Dr Farish had a medium sized leather holdall and a small doctor's bag, the couple's husband lifted their newly-wed heavy cases with ease and Sally realised he was stronger than he looked. She gathered her shawl about her and shivered.

Dr Farish was tucking his pocket watch back in his little jacket pocket. 'Do you have a carriage waiting?' he asked the couple.

They assured him they had and they shook hands and the men exchanged business cards.

Sally stood on the platform, there seemed to be several train tracks on both east and west sides of the station, the tracks in the middle had stationary trains. She was aware they had arrived through a tunnel, looking back at the tunnel it seemed very distant and hardly visible etched in the background.

The black bricks beneath her feet seemed to be moving, they glittered here and there with white frost. The red-black walls behind them were adorned with advertising tin posters: soap; cigarettes; cocoa and tea.

'Come, Mrs Mayhew, Dr Farish ordered.

'What?'

'I can't leave you stranded. Please, this way.'

She heard a whistle's loud peeeep. People were milling around them, all with somewhere to go, people to see, black figures amongst black stone and tunnels. There was an echo about the place which was quite unearthly.

Sally was moving in the direction of everyone else and she was so very tired. A bench looked inviting.

'Come, this way.' Dr Farish opened a small gate. Before she knew it she was standing outside a large impressive entrance to the station. Down the road was a line of horses and carriages, the horses were quiet, hanging their heads were they stood, trying to sleep where they were standing, cold air escaped their nostrils steaming up into the blackness. Sally wanted to stroke them all, reassure them, and where was all this caring coming from? She'd had her laudanum on the train just before the train pulled in, she'd smuggled her bag into the ladies and downed her measure like a man might down a brandy. The urge to have another had been too overwhelming to resist, she had a second dose spontaneously. It occurred to her she might never reach her children, she might disappear forever and they'd never know where she was.

She had a vague recollection of the train station being built when she'd been a nanny taking a trip out with the little boy in her charge. They'd had tea and cakes somewhere, they must have passed the tea room inside, she wanted to ask Dr Farish if it was still there.

Where was he taking her? Why was she letting him usher her into this carriage? Why was she leaning against the carriage window being covered over with a horsey-smelling blanket? She pulled the blanket about her and up over her face, so nobody could see her. She liked the darkness, the way she could breathe steady with the clip-clop of horse's hooves.

Chapter Fourteen

Nicholas had been responding to a plea for help in retrieving several horses that had escaped from a stable and were running rampant through the streets, yet if he thought about it, the horses would most likely have found their way back to their stables when hunger kicked in.

As he looked from Alice (who had ran up to him excitedly and kissed him affectionately on both cheeks) to Charlotte, who stood back, tall and pale, overwhelmed that she had found her little brother, he wondered what thoughts swam in her head.

How did Charlotte know Alice? Charlotte had told him that she didn't know anyone in London. Had she lied to him? She was breath-taking, yet she wore an expression of puzzlement. He wanted to explain about his relationship with Alice but he couldn't explain here in this cold damp air in front of anyone else, especially with Alice standing here in animated excitement.

Chasing the swift silhouette of Henry and watching him disappear into a dark alley had left him out of breath. He put his hands in his pockets and caressed the seven-way knife and slipped the blade closed. Would he have used it on Henry? God help him if he had.

The Thames was filled with dark water, several swans swam by, and they looked like they sailed down the river in sleep. Swans? He wanted to ask Tom where the swans had come from. Tom struck a match and lit his pipe; he was a tall man leaning over the river wall waiting to be told what to do next.

Charlotte was calm. He could see it in her eyes. He couldn't touch her, he couldn't hold her hand but he could say her name.

'Charlotte.' His breast ached as if her stare crushed against is heart. 'The night is full of coincidences,' he said. He could hear the undertones of the river water as it twisted and meandered, and he thought of his aunt asleep in his house.

'Does Aunt Mary know where you are?'

A gas lamp flickered as its wicker surged, and then it glowed bright and steady.

Charlotte looked at him as if to say, '*What do we do now? Who cares about your Aunt Mary?*'

'You all right, Peter?' Will asked again.

'Yer should not 'ave come back for me. Thanks.'

The tall filthy boy had been ready to risk his life for him. Will would be eternally grateful, but he should never had let Peter try to fool Henry, he should be brave enough to fight his own battles or at the very least, stood by Peter's side from the outset.

'I shouldn't have let you talk me into it in the first place,' he said.

'We look out for kids around 'ere,' said Peter.

'I'm not a kid,' answered Will.

'No, I guess you're not,' said Peter.

'This is Peter,' said Will, introducing him to everyone.

Nicholas realised Will had been talking. Had the boy ran off and got himself into trouble again? Had Charlotte heard what Will had been saying? He let his gaze linger on her eyes.

'Look, Peter has to stay with us,' continued Will. 'I insist. When you hear what Peter did for me you'll agree.'

'You're in no position to barter,' said Nicholas. 'Peter can stay on the 'Merganser'. Tom can organise food and a bed.'

'But he's my friend,' pleaded Will, as if Peter was some new commodity.

'And you, Nicholas. Shall you come back to my house with us?' asked Alice.

He thought of the stare of the tiger and the clashing of antlers on the walls.

'It would be better if you rode back with us,' added John. 'They can explain to you what has happened in the carriage.'

'Yes, yes, of course,' he answered.

'I'll come back for you, Peter,' said Will. 'You'll love it on the captain's boat. Tom will feed you and sort you out a bath, won't you Tom.'

Tom laughed and nodded.

'Let's go then,' said Alice.

And Nicholas wondered if Charlotte would sleep in, in the morning, or if she would sleep at all, or if she would cry or slip away at dawn when everyone else was sleeping.

'Nicholas, don't look so worried, mother and father are away at the country house,' said Alice.

'Will, why did you run off again? Why didn't you talk to me? I thought we were good?'

'Char – I—'

'Why go to Alice's house and end up at the docks? Why put me through all that? Was it Henry? Did he threaten you again?'

'No – I was going back to the boat for your birthday present. I left it behind and I wanted it for today. Then I realised Henry was following me and I met Peter, he offered to help me but it didn't work.' Will couldn't tell Charlotte about Nicholas and Alice, not on her birthday and certainly not when Alice was looking at him like he was a foolish boy. He would wait a day at least.

'Oh, Will …'

All summer Henry had seen Sally's health improve, and in the Autumn it was as if she had returned in her mind, some days she looked at him like she really saw him, not the conniving, double dealing and how many times he could con someone into buying a keg of brandy, no, it was as if she saw how he worried he was that he might not sell anything or worse, not have any to sell, that the sea might empty of all the fish and the sands empty of all the crabs. And in seeing him she'd see another line form on his brow, and so he'd sail out to sea again and gain another cat's claw around his eyes.

It was nice to have someone look at you and ask for nothing. He'd give anything to Sally and the kids without wishing for anything in return, yet when he thought about it, the girl always laid an extra plate if he was there, even when Sally had been out of it. For years Sally had been out of it.

He had always left a keg of brandy in Sally's larder and most nights after supper he had sat down by their fire and downed a glass or two before heading back to his room in the boarding house.

The girl didn't communicate with him much, she'd serve up food as if he were a guest, then she'd go off to the kitchen and do one of her chores, or she'd read to Will, or silently to herself, and then she'd most likely take Will to bed. Sometimes he thought she was grateful to him for sitting with Sally. They'd grown into this routine; he'd grown into this family not sure if they really wanted him or needed him. But want was a different thing from need.

He slid through the leaning church gate. It had been a long walk from the docks. He probably should go back to his room at the inn, but he was curious, and you never know, the mudlark boy might come back here, he wanted a word with that boy.

Henry looked up at the bell tower, the bell was missing. The night sky though, was full of stars. He sensed something behind him and shivered, when he turned a large black horse lifted its head and looked in his direction. The horse must have wandered in through the broken wall.

He had nothing to give the horse so he ignored it. He needed to wake up the Reverend. He began to knock loudly on the ancient door, and he bellowed loud enough to wake the dead.

Ribbons of yellow light fluttered from behind arched windows on the cold winter's night. As if light could be a gift! Henry chastised his romantic notions but couldn't help wonder at it, and when the creaking door opened and the Reverend stood there all in black, candelabra glowing, all the pent up rage went out of him.

'What is it? Oh, it's you again. Henry isn't it?'

'Are you hiding 'im?' Henry blurted out. He noticed the Reverend's shock white pallor, the lines etched on his brow, his thinning long white hair and sideburns, there were decades of caring on the old face.

'You're not lost? Or hurt?'

'No. I'm looking for a boy. A mudlark.'

'Well there are plenty of them here. What do you want with the boy? Has he stolen from you?'

'No. I owe 'im. I want to give 'im something.'

'Money? Food?'

'Aye,' said Henry, thinking on his feet. 'I knew his mother.'

'Who do you think was his mother? That'll help identify him.'

Henry said the first name that came into his head, his mother's name, 'Mabel Card.'

'Come inside. That your horse?'

'Thanks. No, he's not my horse.'

The Reverend nodded knowingly. Henry blundered inside, eyes as black as a shrimps. If there was such a thing as faith he could do with some right now.

'None of the children here have mothers. Not mothers that will take them in anyway. Mabel did take a boy in before she died. I should have told you that before when you came to see me. He was such a little thing then, and such a little thing when she died, then he grew out of all proportion, at least he had a few years with a proper roof over his head. But he's not here, I warned Peter, *If you don't get back before nightfall you're locked out for the night*! I have to take care of the little ones you see.'

His own mother had taken in the mudlark! She always 'ad a soft spot she did. Did that mean the mudlark lad Peter was some sort of kin?

'This is for 'im. Clothe 'im and feed 'im for as long as it lasts.' His mother didn't need a gravestone. She'd be better pleased with this gesture of two gold sovereigns to feed the boy.

'And afterwards, when it's run out?'

'I'll be back,' said Henry. He was standing just inside the church beside a small font decorated with holly wreaths around its base and greenery from mistletoe drooping from its basin, unlit candles protruding from it into the darkness; the moisture from his breath wound up to great stone arches.

'Yer've no saints at yer windows?'

'Funds don't stretch that far.'

He omitted to say with all these mouths to feed, thought Henry.

'How many kids do yer feed?'

'It varies. It should get better soon. It is improving. The little ones get school every day and people make donations for their lunches. You have to have faith.'

'Faith in God or the new laws?'

'Both. Does it matter? You're here now.'

'And I'm an act of God?' Henry suddenly perplexed by his donation, thought the kids might be better left to fend for themselves like he had had too, otherwise they would get soft and dependent on others.

'Before Mabel died she said the lad reminded her of a boy she'd lost.'

'Yer said is name was Peter? She took in just the one boy right?'

'As far as I know.

'Thank the Lord for that,' said Henry. He knew who the boy was now. He knew his name and he knew why he was so conniving.

'Bless you,' said the Reverend.

Henry chuckled at the very idea, and then he turned for the long walk back to Summerville House. He'd see if Charlotte was there. Warn her against marrying a man she hardly knew. Ask the girl what she was up to sending Will off into the night like that.

When he saw the horse waiting for him he took it as an omen.

The road seemed endless when most of the city was sleeping. Thin fog and long lanes, and so many bridges, where, if he was honest, Henry thought he might slip from the horse's back and drop into a dark gurgling river. The horse however, continued to clip-clop despite its apparent exhaustion and drooping his head every now and sometimes even stopping and nodding off where he stood.

Henry talked to the horse, he told him to stick to his guns and to keep on track, to aspire for better things, for a better contract or a better owner. The horse in turn pricked up his ears and continued to carry Henry on his journey to an area he was not particularly familiar with but had gained knowledge of from his enquiries at the inn. And so the road to Summerville House unravelled. Henry learnt what it was to ride bareback on cobbles, the slippery bridges and run-of-the-mill shoddy roads.

The moon came out as they approached Summerville House. White light lit up the house's pearly exterior – like cream against the bare-black branches in the garden where Henry wondered if he could tether the horse he was now fond of. The horse flicked his tail as Henry slid from his back. Henry watched the horse's breath and put a hand on his rump which was hot to his cold touch. Henry could hardly mutter a word to the beast now, he was so tired and his mouth was frozen over. The horse had given him an interlude into which he had escaped from bartering, robbing or conniving. He patted the horse's rear and watched him walk away. He hoped the horse headed for a warm stable and plenty of hay.

Contrary to what he thought people might think of him (shifty, with darting eyes and a wonky nose) Henry had never broken into a house. Barns and outbuildings were different. A house was private, a house had people and personal things, and women. Not women like his mother who would have probably welcomed an intruder and given them a cut price, or women like Sally who most probably wouldn't be aware of them. No, most houses had proper women or lasses, like the girl, feisty, but at the sight of a robber most women would be frightened, and he didn't want to frighten anyone again, so therefore, he had to be quiet.

He walked around the back of the house. He thought it was a grand house. He counted over thirty steps for the length of it before he was distracted by a dog barking somewhere upstairs. Whether it was his smell or his coat rattling he couldn't be sure, perhaps both. He leaned on a wall, and then he slithered down to a squatting position and rested his head on his hands. How had he come to be here? What drove him? Why had he left Cromer where he had everything under control? How had he let the lass lead him to this? It wasn't like they were real kin. He tried to move his frozen lips and then thought, actually they were kind of kin. Then he heard a soft whinny; the horse had returned and stood in front of him.

'Stupid begger,' he muttered.

The horse was lost and the horse was cold, reels of breath escaped from his nostrils.

A window opened above him.

'Who are you? What do you want?'

Henry got up and stepped into view so he could see the stranger and the stranger see him.

'I'm Henry Card. Charlotte and Will's soon-to-be-stepfather. I'd come to speak to them. I have a message from their mother.' He was quite pleased with himself. He'd gain entry into the house without having to break in after all.

He patted the horse.

'He seems to have wandered into your garden. Should we cover him with a blanket and give him some apples and a bucket of water, put in him in your shed perhaps? He's freezin'.'

The window closed. In a few minutes Henry could give some more spiel and a bit of flattery and find out what Charlotte was up too.

It wasn't heaven. Sally knew this because of the smell of disinfectant. The smell made her want to sneeze but as she tried to lift her hand to her face she found they were tied to the bed. Dear God, she was strapped to a bed?

Sally kept her eyes tight shut. Instinct kicked in. If she feigned sleep or unconsciousness, she could work out what to do about her situation before any doctor arrived for she was sure she was in a hospital of some sort.

She wondered if her suffering for John's loss would ever be over and if she might lie here for weeks or months. She heard voices, but undecipherable words, perhaps they were whispering about her? The bed linen that covered her was crispy, there was a pillow of feathers beneath her head. Only a few days ago Charlotte had thumped her pillow and shaken down the feathers, '*Mother, will you dress again today?*'

She lay still with her face on the pillow and her lips pressed tightly together, she must not cry, she must not make a sound.

Other noises began to filter in. Someone gasped, someone else began to hum a bad tune, someone coughed; at least she wasn't alone here. She made a fist with her hands and pulled hard against the restraints.

Someone must have undressed her, she wore a strange gown and beneath it she was naked. Something was wrong, an unaccounted for smell, some unknown soap reeked from her body. She swallowed. Her mouth was dry. She was hot. She had a sudden need to pass water.

A woman's hysterical voice from only a few feet away began to cry, 'Him, him, him, him!'

Sally wanted to sleep, to slip right into her pillow and wake up from this nightmare. If she went to sleep she could do that. Wake up in the carriage. She'd got in a carriage with Dr Farish. The kindly man. They'd got off the train at King's Cross Station.

'Sit back,' Dr Farish had said.

She could taste laudanum in her mouth, sweet, sweet syrup. She had a couple of bottles of it in her bag wrapped in a spare pink shawl. Where was her bag? She ached for a dose, perhaps a cup of tea, a glass of water.

'Him, him, him!'

'Hello, Clara. How are you this morning?'

It was Dr Farish. The medical doctor that deals with examining dead bodies and delivering babies, who diagnoses belly-aches and fevers.

'She's still hysterical.'

'Yes, Doctor. Yesterday she fainted.'

'Has she started eating or drinking yet?'

'Just a nibble here and there.'

'You must get her to eat. Force her.'

Sally heard the sound of a page being turned.

'Yes, Dr Farish. We'll hold her down and get some porridge down her.'

'Good. Do it soon.'

A few moments passed. Sally listened intensely. She felt a sigh in her face.

'This one's had such a fascinating journey. Riding trains at night, going from place to place with no destination. Lucky I was there when she overdosed.'

'Yes, it's a good job you were there.'

'When she wakes up you must give her the dose I've written up or she'll fall more deeply into melancholia.'

'Yes, Dr Farish.'

'Mrs Mayhew!'

He was shaking her shoulder.

He had promised to deliver her to Summerville House, to be with her beautiful Charlotte and Will.

'Mrs Mayhew, open your eyes. I know you're awake.'

Sally wondered about the boats, sailing across the sea at night, sailing into the docks, and there she was, sea-weary, standing on the docks under the stars, a carriage with two black horses waiting to take her to her children.

'I want to go home,' she whispered.

'Open your eyes,' the doctor said.

She imagined a couple of fairies had been sitting on her cheeks last night when she was sleeping, one dressed in pink, one in blue, their gossamer wings closed while they concentrated plaiting and weaving her blonde eyelashes together so that all she could do now was peak at this world through tiny knots and twists.

'I thought you were a kindly man,' she said.

Through tiny gaps she saw his heaviness, it etched his soul. He stood on two hooves; he had grey goats hair down each side of his face.

'Is Mrs Mayhew your real name? Is your first name really Sally?'

'No, my real name is Victoria.'?

'Victoria what?'

'Victoria Saxe-Coburg-Saalfeld.'

The doctor sighed. 'And what was your last address?'

'You know my address. I told you on the train.'

'Tell me again.'

'Fairy Mound Castle, in the blue sky.'

'You're not helping. It would be better for you if you were to co-operate.'

'Why have you tied me up?'

'It's for your own good.

'She can have breakfast and her medication straight after,' he said to the orderly.

Sally opened her eyes fully she had to see what was going on with the ward orderly woman that had taken to working in this place, legs as thin as a sparrows, a pointed beaky face that she could tuck under one arm so she could not see the real world. Despite the blue dress, white apron and white cap that the woman wore her bony shoulders still drooped and she rested her hands on end of the iron bed, she took the book from Dr Farish which he had finished writing in and placed it at the end of her bed securing it with a clip. Sally looked at the sparkling oak floorboards to see if the woman had a shadow, and the shadow uncoiled and raised one arm like a wing salute to Dr Farish. It was then Sally noticed the windows, they were barred but they were at least windows, it was daylight, and the two people at the end of her bed walked away, heads down, whispering. Sally pulled at the restraints again and let out a long agonizing cry.

In Alice's house Charlotte slipped through a door that revealed a large room. Leather bound books, black, red and brown with gold pressed lettering adorned the neat shelves. Charlotte looked up at aged tell-tale signs of pipe-smoking and cigar-smoking, it yellowed the intricate plasterwork of swirls and angles in the wide exuberant cornices. Maroon velvet curtains draped at the window on the far side of the room. She walked towards a mahogany desk which had a red leather insert, two wooden inkwells and a chair that ran on castors, the chair was decorated with a rich carved back. Here and there other things had been placed in the room, a drinks trolley with decanters of brown, red and yellow drinks, the trolley hung heavy with a sweet smell of cherries. The fire-place on the west wall, laid up with a log fire, on its hearth a variety of silver fireside implements ready to stoke, shovel and grasp. Several easy chairs scattered around the room on the thick Indian patterned carpet, tendrils weaving to all corners and the trickle of sunlight brightening its reds, blues and greens.

Charlotte, reluctant to face anyone took a few deep breaths to think about her business, the reason why she had set off for London in the first place. If she got back to the reason then the complicated relationship with Nicholas, this burning inside, this heaviness that made her shoulders droop, that made her fix her stare on the floor, the lost battle, the things she couldn't change, they might all go away and though it would leave her sad and devastated, it was recoverable from at this moment in time.

She had to face reality. Nicholas didn't love her. Nicholas was just being kindly. Nicholas loved Alice, it was obvious from the way he kept looking at her and she him.

There, she'd said it. The truth. She tried to say the words out loud but nothing came out other than 'Nicholas,' in a small voice.

The parrot in the hallway gave a loud squawk; the cover had been lifted off the cage.

To find where breakfast was, she followed the voices. All she had to do was get through the next hour or so, then she could go back to Summerville House, collect her and Will's things and go home. Nicholas could also return her new things to the shop and get his money back and she wouldn't owe him anything but her gratitude. Never-mind the jewels, never-mind her dreams. Well, maybe she could have a quick look around for a jewellers shop before she got the train home. But what if anyone recognised the jewels as being stolen from someone of 'gentry'? Perhaps she was after all, better to keep them a secret. Better to protect her mother.

Alice had everything, the sparkle, the background, the intelligence, why, even kindness. And most of all she had history with Nicholas and a similar background.

She leaned on the carved door of the library. She would just slip away. She hadn't even cried last night when she'd seen the two of them whispering together. She couldn't risk being heard, and lying there in a huge bed in one of Alice's nightgowns, she had known a darkness in the house and the restlessness of everyone in it. Will, on the other hand, was finding adventure with almost every move he made, and she must tell him to slow down, to step back, to wait, for it was her business here and her job to deliver him safely back home and to get back to making her mother well again.

Determined, she went out of the door but paused again as she caught the eyes of the portrait in the hallway. She began to perspire, her heart sounding in her ears, but why? Against the trickle of sunlight through the front door glass she walked closer to the painting.

It was a similar painting to the one in the parlour, the same woman, the same black riding gear. Alice's mother held the horse's reins. She was smiling at the artist as he had swept and coloured in with his brushes. Her hair was as black as Charlotte's. Her eyes were blue like the deepest sky, and there was something unfurling in the shape of her mouth. A word? A whisper? Against a tree lined background Charlotte imagined she was there in the picture and perhaps she heard approaching footsteps as the clouds folded in …

'Charlotte. Happy Birthday!' Will cried. And he rushed down the hallway and took her hand.

He was an affectionate ten-year-old.

'Thank you, Will.'

'I have a present for you. I was going to return last night so it would be there at Summerville House in the morning but then Henry—'

'I know. It's all right.'

Last night before Will had slipped into a huge four-poster bed fit for a king, he had told her again what Henry had said on the docks about the dead man on the beach. They both agreed what Henry said sounded plausible but why chase Will and threaten him? Henry's story didn't wholly add up, especially the injury Henry claimed the man had sustained and the coastguard saying the man had drowned without any other injury.

'Who's this?' asked Will.

'It's Alice's mother.'

'She doesn't look like Alice. She looks like you. It could be you.'

'Perhaps Alice takes after her father.'

'Like I take after mother and you take after father.'

'Just so.'

'Is there a painting of Alice and her brother? I should like to see a picture of them together. I wonder what her brother looks like.'

'They must be in a different part of the house. A private room, maybe the mother's bedroom.'

'Everyone's being so kind aren't they?'

'Yes indeed.'

She took one last glance of the portrait, the wide mouth, a soft wind blowing across Alice's mother's face, blowing her hair. Charlotte was overcome with such a longing, and a thought again of how lucky Alice was, she imagined this woman lifting up a girl child, and holding her with such tenderness that tears came to her eyes.

'Charlotte, come.' Will tugged her hand. 'Let's go home. Do you want to go home? We don't have to stay. I'll say I believe Henry and I'm sure he'll leave me alone. He'd never hurt us.'

Will tapped nervously on a table with his other hand, and glancing down withdrew his hand quickly.

'What is this?'

'Elephants feet – its lower legs.'

'That's gross.'

'Quite so.'

Charlotte wondered if the food tasted better to Will than it did to her. She watched him bite into a sausage, suck up scrambled eggs, lash butter on toasted bread and then he licked his fingers.

The blazing fire heated her cheeks, she was afraid to swallow in case Nicholas and Alice might turn to look at the noise she might make, her naïveté alighting in her watery eyes.

But oh – the song of Alice as she chatted animatedly, her excitement of having her beloved Nicholas at her breakfast table as if no one else was there.

Alice was saying how marvellous her coachman was, how he could do anything, indeed he had helped Minnie cook breakfast. Who was this Minnie, Charlotte had yet to see her. A coachman and a companion cooking breakfast for guests, thought Charlotte, looking at her plate of food in disdain, 'Whatever was the world coming to?' she wanted to say sarcastically. But she could find no fault with the food, it was just the vile taste in her mouth that soured the down-turn-corner of her lips. Oh, her ungratefulness. Alice was wearing a dark green silk dress that pinched tightly at the waist, the dress sleeves draped over the table with layers of cream lace, which was repeated around Alice's heaving (though quite small) bosom. The bodice of the dress had a little jacket-type flair which gathered over the bustle, edged with the same lace. Around her neck she wore a gold chain with a gold locket. And just how had she made her hair up in golden ringlets tucked back behind her ears, so quickly? So beautifully?

Charlotte, was struck dumb in her grey skirt and white blouse as Alice poured tea.

'It'll have to be black tea, we haven't had a milk delivery for a few days, there's something wrong with the cows apparently. It's a bit early for mint tea.'

Charlotte imagined the rhino head on the wall snorted.

Alice offered to carry Nicholas' plate to the dresser – feet away – to get him some more rashers of bacon.

Charlotte heard the tiger's head on the wall growl.

When Alice sat back down after loading his plate, the stuffed red squirrels began to throw nuts at Alice's head.

She must stop with these thoughts, she was thinking like her mother, she must eat something, her head was swimming, she liked Alice, she really did.

'I take it your parents won't be joining us for Charlotte's birthday tonight?' Nicholas asked Alice.

'Of course not. Not even for someone as important as Charlotte. But we'll be there, Minnie and I.'

'It's a shame they can't be here. We have much to discuss,' he said.

'Yes, I suppose we do,' said Alice.

'We keep putting it off,' said Nicholas, turning to look at Charlotte.

What was the matter with him! This girl, this Alice, wouldn't ever sleep in a hammock. Wouldn't ever cook eggs or turn a bed, let alone wash the sheets! Was Alice pressing her leg against Nicholas' under the table! Those big blonde eyelashes fluttered and her bosom heaved. Alice tucked a perfected wisp of loose hair behind her ear.

Charlotte just had to bide her time. The moment Alice knew about the story invented about her and Nicholas it could potentially shatter Alice's little world, the fact that Nicholas could concoct such a story which could greatly embarrass their families.

'Nicholas, I need to speak to you in private,' said Charlotte.

'Bless me! She talks at last!' screeched Alice, jumping back in her chair.

Of course Alice was teasing her, Charlotte knew that but when Nicholas chuckled it was too much. Charlotte stood up and fled the room.

Will watched Nicholas get up and go after Charlotte.

'Should I go after her?' asked Will.

'No. Leave Nicholas to it,' answered Alice.

'But it's her birthday.'

'I know. Nicholas will take care of it. I can see the way she looks at him and me. Do you want to tell me what's going on between those two?'

'No. I can't explain,' said Will, terrified his expression might give something away. He was sure Charlotte and he were leaving soon. They could go back home and forget all this.

'But you know something is going on between those two?'

Will nodded.

'But you won't betray a trust?'

Will nodded again.

'So Charlotte has another secret? Her story gets more intriguing than it is already?'

Will didn't answer.

'I admire your sister. She takes care of you. I imagine her somewhere gutting fish, soothing horses, and later coming home and soothing your mother and getting your supper. Church bells ringing as the sun goes down. I can understand her need for something better for you all but I don't think she appreciates her freedom. She's ducked the system somehow, avoided the streets. At any time when things get bad you pulled together and moved your luckless lives on. I admire that brave quality she has. And don't forget your father saved my father's life. He'd never forgive me if I didn't help you. But besides that, I'm drawn to you.'

Alice was talking to him like he was an adult. Will had to be careful what he said back to Alice. He didn't want to come out with a boy's rambling thoughts. Alice's hands rested on the table. She was more serious than he had ever seen her. Her moods could change so quickly. It was a moment when he wished he wasn't wearing his shoddy gansey, when he was glad he'd washed his face in the basin on the dressing table in his room.

He took a sip of water.

'How are your horses?' he asked randomly.

'They are well. John, goes to the stables every day to make sure they are fed properly and he mucks them out quite often,' she said kindly.

'They are very beautiful horses.'

'Yes, they are. I wonder what Nicholas and Charlotte are talking about.' Alice picked up her teacup, she raised the cup slowly to her lips and sipped the tea without making a noise. Music seemed to flow through her like the rays of the sun shining on her hair.

'You play the piano as well?'

'As well as what?'

'Your wonderful sketches.'

'Ah yes, I have a thing for sketches. It comes from having too many hours to fill.'

'It's more than that. You have a natural gift.'

'Why, thank you, Will.'

'I would appreciate your expertise. Would you spend a few hours teaching me?'

'Of course. But only if you do something for me in return.'

'Of course.'

'Allow me to teach you at your home. Let me visit you and stay a few days to explore your town and get some air. I long for sea air.'

Will gazed around the room. He remembered a phrase Henry used for paying guests and he said, 'We are humble people but honest and clean, and you will never be cold or hungry while you stay with us.'

'Deal,' said Alice, putting her cup down and holding out her hand.

'Deal,' Will replied, taking her hand in his. He sighed, he could pretend for a while longer.

Charlotte stood by the window in the library. She'd struggled with her hair earlier in her room until finally she had simply made one long plait. She wished she was proficient with her hair the way that Alice was, for when Nicholas came in she wondered if she looked childlike.

Oh my, he approached her with such an intense look his blue eyes seared right into her, could he hear her beating heart?

'Oh, Nicholas …'

'Charlotte …'

He stood close to her, just gazing down at her, he was so tall. For goodness sake his white shirt was open at the neck.

'What's the matter,' he asked.

Was that tension surging through his entire body?

He reached for her hand. It was as if a fire had reached inside her and made her heart roar.

'Oh, my dear,' he said.

He would have kissed her but she dropped his hand and turned away.

'No, we mustn't, not here. Not—'

'I need to explain something to you. It's all so complicated. I made a promise to Alice, years ago.'

'Promise? What promise?'

'I have to talk to Alice first and then I'll explain everything.'

'About your promise, about our lie …' Charlotte was trembling.

'Oh my little mermaid, can't you see how—'

'I can see how it would break Alice's heart. I shall go now. I'll take Will to Summerville House and collect our things, we will go home. I'm so sorry for all of this, for interfering in your lives.'

'Charlotte, you don't understand. Listen to me.' His hand burnt into her arm.

'Please don't …' She knew if she turned around to him she would fall into his arms. Suddenly the door burst open,

'Oranges, oranges, oranges!'

Startled, Charlotte turned to look at who could only be Minnie. She was about the same height as Aunt Mary, she had the same plumpness around her middle, her hair was greying, and tied up in a knot. Minnie must be a nickname, thought Charlotte, for this woman had a small nose, small black eyes and pursed lips, she held her hands in front of her like begging paws. She was heading for the decanters, obviously for the cherry liquor, which her eyes flickered to first, and them they came back to rest on the pair of them. She wore a crisp white apron over a full brown skirt and white blouse, she moved her hands and gripped the white bib of the apron.

'Oh my goodness,' she said, studying Charlotte. Minnie was staring at her like she was a ghost, her rosy pallor turned white, she opened her mouth.

'Minnie? What's the matter?' asked Nicholas.

'It can't be!'

'What is it, Minnie?'

Minnie was swooning. And Nicholas rushed towards her but not in time to stop her before she hit her head on the elephant's feet table top.

The side of Minnie's face made a loud thud.

'I'll get help, and towels!' cried Charlotte. She acted on instinct. She ran to tell Alice and Mrs Johnson. She found John in the kitchen and asked him to fetch a doctor. John responded instantly. Then she found a bowl, filled it with water and gathered a few towels.

Nicholas was carrying Minnie in his arms into the parlour, Alice opened the door, and Will arranged cushions on the settee.

Charlotte kneeled on the floor beside Minnie and applied a cold compress to the wound, curbing the blood flow.

'Luckily it's a small gash,' she said. 'Though so much blood. She's stirring, and that's a good sign, isn't it?'

'My goodness,' said Alice, biting her lip. 'I knew I should have hidden the liquor. She's been getting worse lately.'

'The bleeding is subsiding,' said Charlotte.

Minnie opened her eyes, it was then Charlotte noticed they were brown, not black.

Minnie raised her small hand and cupped Charlotte's face, she whispered, 'Beautiful child, you have returned after all these years. You found your way home.'

Sally opened her eyes under the dark shadow of Dr Farish. She didn't remember walking to the hard chair she found she was sitting on. Her wrists were bound to the arms of the chair. She studied the chair arms, oak maybe, chopped and sawn from long life in woodland.

She heard a noise like a cat that had strayed into another cat's territory, a long strangled mew, she knew it was her own voice. She didn't look at the doctor for his reaction because she was willing her wrists to slip out of the binds, and coaxing her body to flex and manoeuvre and float to the ceiling. Let her body take to the air. Let her be an angel in white suspended high up by the ceiling. That would shock Dr Farish.

She tried to pick up the chair and walk away with it. The chair was nailed to the floor.

Her feet were bare. Her ankles were numb, her blood had pooled in them. She stretched and flexed her ankles and beat her heels on the wooden floorboards. Her feet were responsive, she pressed her heels down harder.

'The fact is – she passed out on the dose you gave her. Could the laudanum be of a different purity?' asked the bird orderly.

Sally took a peek at Dr Farish.

'I wonder if the person who supplies her has been watering it down, quite methodically and slowly, because the fact is she sunk so low as to be positively comatose.'

Sally's hands were cold. How sad they looked, dry and thin with chipped nails of different lengths. How her hands trembled. She wanted to write a letter to those she loved. She wanted to write where she was staying and that she was sorry for how she'd been and that she loved them. How she would change and be the mother she used to be if only she could get home again.

Sally lifted her face up just enough meet Dr Farish's scrutiny. He fell silent. Wherever this place was, whatever room she was in, also fell silent. The audience was holding its breath. There a flicker in Dr Farish that went deeper than the surface of his blinking eyelids. Could he be thinking he might have made a mistake? An error of judgement? And then the flicker slipped away. Someone in the room began slopping the floor from a cold bucket of water. The audience let out long deep breaths. The ladies down either side of a long room were all shackled at the wrists, she looked from one to the other into the pools of their lost, dark eyes. They hummed, *Welcome to this spacious dwelling, where the ambient temperature is pleasant most of the time, where you will be served the insides of animals on green leaves, where you may write letters and maps on the ceiling, so that the hours you spend shackled you can look upwards and become educated, it should be so time consuming to read and study the ceiling that the days will pass in a jiffy.*

Sally thought it would be such fun to paint a mural of the sea-bed, maybe Happisburgh sands with the shipwrecks swaying and decaying, and the gulls as they swoop and dive for silver fish. Oh, to paint a tall ship – all its sails billowing, and embarking from the ship (where it is safely anchored) would be John, smiling in the sunlight, the north wind lifting his hair, a herring gull on his shoulder.

'I, should like to write a letter,' she said in a faint voice. She looked directly at Dr Farish.

The bird orderly with him took a sharp intake of breath.

'Sally, a letter you say?'

'Yes.'

'And why would someone like you want to write a letter? To whom would you write a letter?'

'My family. I should like to write to my family. I think I told you my address on the train. Could there have been some confusion?'

'No confusion on my part.' He stroked his long grey fuzzy sideburns.

'I think perhaps I must have been confused,' she said.

'How's that, Sally?'

'In trusting you.'

Behind all his facial hair, his face reddened.

'You melancholy women, you're lucky to have me,' he spoke so quietly it was almost under his breath.

And then Sally was struck by the thought that she couldn't map her way home because she didn't know where she was, her children didn't know where she was, and nor did Henry, and it might be a week or even until after Christmas (or if ever?) that they would return home and find her missing.

Sally lowered her head in submission, she must be more careful, if she had to find a way out of here she had to gain Dr Farish's trust, not anger him. Christmas was coming, the goose was getting fat. She was staring into his round middle parts, she lowered her eyes again, blinked them tight shut.

'This is the day room,' he said to her. 'Not a bad little room considering.' And to the bird orderly he said, 'Give her three quarters a dose, water it down and monitor her reaction to it. If we get it right and we can experiment to try and cut it down even more, even off it all together.'

Sally heard the bedroom door slam. John was angry. It was dark, and they'd argued in whispers, cursing, (he more than she) so as not to wake the children. John had been angry with her he'd been repeating something about promises. She'd said they'd had to keep the promise because the truth was too painful to bear.

The jewels were still there in the top of the travel box. She adorned herself in gold chains and diamond necklaces, chains around her wrists, and a tiara on her head. She was laughing at him now. He was outside at the window turning out his pockets, empty of gold coins. With a puzzled expression he began to speak through the glass but she couldn't hear him. She put her face against the glass, he was saying something about a birthday … her cold breath spread on the glass, she wiped at it. John was gone, she looked out amongst so much grey, and the sea was creeping under the window in the yard where he had stood.

'Mrs Mayhew! Sally!'

Sally opened her eyes, she was in a chair and her hands were still bound to it. She looked across to the woman's voice.

'Remember where you are? Take a long deep breath. We're getting out of here soon. I promise. You were having another bad dream,' said the woman who was force-fed. She was more ghostly looking than Sally herself could ever remember being, white hair hung starkly around the woman's gaunt face, she was so bony it was frightening, her wrists bones protruded like hardened pegs.

'There's nothing to be afraid of, they mean no harm. Do-gooders up themselves that's all.'

'He kidnapped me.'

'Yes, 'spect he did. No-one can come and get you then? That's the nuts and bolts of it. He's trying to put us back together again. Some of us, well, we don't want to be put back together, and we just want to float off. It's his opinions that's all, see? He and them there so called assistants have different opinions to us he's kidnapped.'

'You too?'

'Maybe.'

Sally glanced at all the misery. What difference would the absence of these women make to anyone? The woman beggar on the street; the prostitute that lived from hand to mouth; the young girl hated by her stepmother; the elderly that had nobody.

'Yes, you're beginning to get the drift. They're not rattling their chains. They fill this place and hold it together. Do you understand?'

'He's made up a story about me that isn't true,' said Sally.

'Then you have a chance, my dear. Just be careful of the dark.'

'What do you mean?'

'It's a long ways off yet.

'Not so long,' said Sally.

'Some days we have recreation,' said the woman. 'That's what you look forward to. I'll get you out of here I promise.'

Nicholas was filled with a sense déjà vu. For some reason he remembered sliding into the stagnant school pond and dragging out James, Alice's brother. They must have been aged ten or thereabouts. James had been thrashing on his back tangled in green weeds and sinking in lily pads. With mud up to his thighs he'd dragged James onto the bank and flaked out beside his friend. Flies had been humming and the bullies had been laughing at them. An angled face of a school master had appeared over them with the sound of retreating footfall.

There, he'd thought, it was out in the open now, the bullies had been found out. It would all be sorted. But the hushed school rooms were only temporary, James and he weren't to know that at the time and all they foresaw for the future were the peaceful long hot days of summer. He had wanted to protect James from the bullies but came to realise they would always be around the corner waiting … you couldn't always protect those you cared about.

'What do you mean, Minnie?' asked Alice, leaning closer to Minnie.

'Surely you can see?' the woman replied.

But Alice could not see because Alice did not know, because Alice was listening with her ear to Minnie's mouth. Charlotte held a towel on Minnie's head wound.

'She may be delirious?' said Charlotte.

'Yes. Quite so,' answered Alice.

Nicholas saw a tremble in Alice's lips as she spoke. Perhaps she'd heard the stories about her mother and the new baby, perhaps in whispers by the maids, perhaps James, who would have been six at the time he heard a baby cry, a mother's screaming, a rush of skirts, slamming doors, raised voices. Perhaps that was why James had been sent away to school. Perhaps Alice aged three, had a memory locked away, or perhaps she had no memory of it at all.

Nicholas had recognised the pearls set in gold around Alice's mother's neck in the hallway.

Minnie was reaching out to touch Charlotte's braids as if they were something precious.

'Your hair is exactly like your mother's was, and her blue eyes, oh so determined, back then.'

Charlotte withdrew the towel from Minnie's head and put the compress in the hands of Alice. 'Hold it here, until the doctor arrives,' she said. 'I should leave. I don't want to be responsible for this woman's delirium.'

'We need you here,' said Nicholas. Charlotte was more than apt at looking after someone injured, he wasn't sure if Alice was, she could start swooning at any minute given her white face. Or maybe Alice saw the resemblance too, it was uncanny when you compared Charlotte's image with that in the portrait of the young Kathryn Merryweather.

'In my father's house, we are surrounded on all sides by dead things, they stare at us. The parrot squawks and we all jump. Yet the parrot doesn't even have a name. He isn't allowed one. I'm surprised he hasn't been stuffed already. I think my father is just waiting for him to die so he can have him stuffed as well.

There's a sadness about my mother, it's embedded in her. I have heard her weep at night so many times. It's not that she doesn't love James and me. I know she does. But when the baby died it was like some part of her heart had been torn away.

You look like her, Charlotte. I can see why Minnie thinks you might be the child that died.'

Nicholas was torn between wanting to gather Charlotte up and protect her, and his admiration for Alice for not over-reacting.

'Charlotte, be a dear, would you see what happened to the tea Mrs Johnson was making.

Goodness know how long the doctor will be,' Alice said.

Nicholas thought, that in Alice's eyes, the idea of Charlotte being the lost child was impossible. But the idea of it for him was growing momentum, he could hear it in the ticking grandfather clock, he could see it fluttering in Minnie's eyelashes as they filled up with love and tears. He'd seen it in Mrs Johnson too, that same flicker of recognition.

'Will, go with your sister. Give us a few minutes,' he said.

Will let out a long sigh and scuttled off.

'I'm proud of you, Alice.'

'Yes, well, we don't need any complications. They don't seem like gold diggers do they? I trust them I do. What do you think, Nicholas?'

'Gold diggers? The idea never once occurred to me. She does look like your mother.'

'It's a coincidence!' Alice shouted in Minnie's face.

'It's Charlotte's birthday today,' Nicholas added, in a supportive way.

'There you see,' said Alice, in a raised voice. 'The baby died a soon after it was born. The dates don't match.'

Minnie's eyes flickered open with a degree of consciousness, she raised her paw like hand and attempted to pat Alice on her arm. Alice caught her hand with her free one and placed it on Minnie's heaving chest.

'Today's date is the day they took her away, dear,' Minnie said. 'They kept the poor little mite quiet in the servants' quarters until they left.'

Alice shivered.

'I'll stoke the fire,' said Nicholas.

'Thank you,' said Alice. She reached for a chequered blanket from the back of the settee and tucked it over Minnie.

'Did you ever hear any stories about your mother's jewels being stolen – or sold?' asked Nicholas.

'Not that I can recall. Why?'

Nicholas picked up the poker and shuffled the red glowing embers before putting a couple of shovelful's of coal on them, which made the room chill even further.

The doctor was tall and thin with a long black moustache, he looked sleepy, perhaps he had nodded off in the carriage parked outside, thought Charlotte. She had sidled up closer to the door leading from the kitchen see the doctor and to hear any conversations the better.

Nicholas greeted the doctor in the hallway. Instead of getting straight to the patient the doctor recited a story that the Queen and the Royal Family were getting ready to spend Christmas at Osbourne, and that Princess Louise was much better.

'Yes, that's good news,' Nicholas said politely.

'One wonders what Prince Albert would have made of the war between France and Germany if he was still alive,' continued the doctor. 'There's an exhibition on for the 'distressed peasantry in France' at the Suffolk Street Studios in Pall Mall if you get the chance. The war does damage, Mr O'Rourke. Have you ever visited France in more pleasant times?'

'Indeed I have, Doctor. Indeed I have.'

'Sad times indeed.'

The doctor had by now shuffled out of his hat and coat and handed them to Nicholas.

'Here I am distributing leaflets advertising the exhibition to all my patients and their families.'

'Let's go and see the patient then,' said Nicholas.

'Of course.'

Nicholas pocketed the leaflet to look at later. There was more chatter in the parlour as the doctor said pretty much the same thing to Alice. Charlotte had followed them into the parlour. He was leaning over Minnie examining her wound.

'Our guests are from Cromer,' said Alice. 'I hear you visited recently?'

'Yes indeed! Splendid place. We were there on our honeymoon!'

'And you visited Cromer?' replied Alice, as if it were such a strange place for a honeymoon.'

'It was wonderful. Fresh crisp sea air, cliff-top walks, woodlands, plenty of shops for my new wife to browse. It is – very quaint.'

'Doctor, please, the patient,' Charlotte butted in.

'Of course,' he replied lingering a tiny bit too long on meeting her gaze.

Minnie was staring at her again. It was easy to see that the woman was not as badly injured as they had first thought. It must have been all the blood that caused them all to get into a panic, she deduced, and hurried out of the room and the stares. She would fetch the tea from Mrs Johnson, even if the woman was acting strangely towards her, it must be catching, all this confusion.

Somehow, Charlotte had been swept along with Alice's wishes to celebrate her birthday. Perhaps Alice was bored, thought Charlotte, and wanted something to fill her time, or perhaps she genuinely needed a friend and the discovery that her father had saved Alice's father's life meant she was attempting some sort of pay back between the families? Whatever her reasons there had been a rushed (on Alice's part) to organise everyone and everything back to Summerville House, and though they'd protested because of Minnie's injury and all the commotion it had caused, Alice still insisted they all return to Nicholas' house.

The thought then occurred to Charlotte that Alice secretly just wanted her out of the house to stop everyone going up to the portrait of Alice's mother and then looking at Charlotte like she was a ghost about to reveal haunting secrets.

She had protested again against exposing Minnie to the long and cold journey, all her protesting was lost on Alice. A small voice then, hushed by Alice, pushed by Alice, and ordered by Alice. And in the hallway while she was waiting on something, Nicholas had caught her staring at the portrait of Alice's mother again.

'The doctor said to feed Minnie up on pig's liver.'

She knew he had been trying to raise a smile from her but she said, 'I should leave here now and go home, everything is getting complicated, it was never meant to become complicated.'

Nicholas had turned away and poked his finger in the parrot cage.

'We need to talk,' he'd said.

'When?' She was drawn to stand closer to him to hear what else he had to say.

'Tonight, after dinner. We'll all talk then. This is why I want Alice there. We need to tell her what's been happening between us.'

'Why? Why Alice particularly?' she'd asked.

Before he could answer Alice had come rushing in and gabbled something about the exhibition and how she couldn't wait to get out of the house and visit his Aunt Mary.

And so here they were, the others were gathered around the table at Summerville House discussing Henry, or the disappearance of Henry not long after his Aunt Mary had provided Henry with breakfast (they had all been in search of any sign of him or anything missing from the house) and she heard Aunt Mary say, 'Such a nice man, so pleasant and charming.' And they didn't say anything different so as not to alarm her.

Charlotte stood next to Nicholas by the sideboard, the beef on a serving plate was bloody; Nicholas carved it easily. The potatoes were crispy; Mrs Johnson had sprinkled them with something, salt, Charlotte realised. At her feet Skip wagged his little tail.

'He didn't find them then?'

'What?'

'You know who I mean and what I mean. Where did you hide them?'

'*Gather ye rosebuds* …' Charlotte had hid the jewels in the piano and had taken them out of the piano when no one was around on their return to the house. A smell of old wood and dust had sprung at her, she had hid soft string bag right at the bottom in the corner of the instrument. She had plucked a string, listened to its long quiver and then put back the bottom board covering the strings.

'I wonder if Henry is outside watching from somewhere.'

'I don't know.' The way Nicholas's eyes sparkled and crinkled when he stood so close, she wished she were alone in the house with him …

'Do you still have the rope swing?' Alice asked and moved in on them with a whir, pointing to the back garden. 'Remember, Nicholas, how we played on that swing. Back and forth we went all summer.'

Nicholas paused for a moment and said, 'As I remember it, you played with your dolls while James and I fired arrows at them.'

'Beasts,' she laughed.

'Aye,' said Nicholas. He picked up the plate of meat he had carved and took it over to the table.

'Sit down, dear Charlotte. We are dying to give you your birthday presents but we must eat first. Come, I'm starving.' Charlotte was aware that Alice was once again, summing her up.

At the table Nicholas was telling Will about his life at sea. 'When you're on a boat in the ocean you want to be seen but only by the right people. You want to be fast. I've sailed as fast as the fastest wind, as far as the furthest sea. I have sailed under all the stars. I have watched dolphins, I've seen pods of dolphins flying out of the sea. I've been with my men in the sea swimming with dolphins, going with the current, listening to the dolphins' crackles and their laughing. I have stroked dolphins, they are the mermaids of the sea. I have seen them round up a million fish, swim up through the middle of them and feast on them. I have seen the so-called unicorns. Really they are narwhals, seal-whale-dolphin type creatures that sing across artic waters. Aye, Will, whalers trap them and bring back their coiled tusks for the Royal scientists to display in museums to keep the unicorn myth alive.

'People, the merchants, the bankers, the politicians, the market stall holders, the shopkeepers, and all the others that travel by train and carriage will come to the exhibition to see a unicorn horn. Aye, all fooled. How much do they pay to see these things, how much is it worth to keep a fantasy alive?

'There's other curiosities abound at this exhibition, see the leaflet the doctor left, stones that have grown in men's kidneys and livers, sea-shells galore, unborn creatures preserved in liquid in bottles, carvings from elephant tusks, artwork, stuffed birds and lions.

'But I tell you, Will, nothing takes your breath away as to see those poor creatures alive. The experience changes you.'

'And afterwards,' asked Charlotte. 'How do you come down from such an experience?'

'You look forward to the next one,' Nicholas laughed.

'You have so many wonderful memories. I can only imagine such things.'

'Then we shall all go to the exhibition together and re-create the story behind the artefacts,' he said.

'Well, it won't be the same,' said Alice. 'And I'm afraid it's us women-folk that get the short straw on adventures. But soon, I shall venture as far as Cromer,' she winked at Will. 'And now it's time for the birthday girl to open her presents,' Alice beamed, producing a brown parcel tied with a pretty green ribbon, which turned out to be a pair of soft brown leather gloves. 'For your poor hands,' said Alice proudly.

The gloves were beautiful but the last comment made Charlotte aware of her status, and what was Alice saying about visiting Cromer? Will interrupted her thoughts by presenting his gift carefully wrapped in brown paper and tied with string.

'Oh, Will, thank you so much my darling boy.'

Will grinned widely. 'You can write your recipes in it,' he said.

'And you'll help me with the drawings?'

'Of course.'

'It is the best present I have ever received,' said Charlotte.

'I went shopping with Tom when you went shopping with Nicholas,' he said innocently.

Charlotte thought he must have retrieved his gift for her from the boat for that had been his reason for leaving the house in secret. But he never made it back to the boat did he? Hadn't they gone straight to Alice's house after finding him? Perhaps Tom had brought the gift to the house while she'd been sleeping, either that or she hadn't got the full story.

Alice looked startled by Will's comment, as if she was aware of some intimacy growing between her and Nicholas that she wasn't in on.

Charlotte twisted a strand of her loose hair. Alice's generosity went beyond the gift of the gloves, her generosity was in her trust and loyalty, it was in heaps and mounds. If it hadn't been for Alice she might never have found Will so soon. Charlotte had never come across such a bright, pretty, helpful girl in all her life. And they rewarded her with secrets and lies. Her hands fidgeted, she folded them on her lap beneath the table.

'You two went shopping together?' asked Alice.

'Given the situation it was quite a normal thing to do don't you think?' said Aunt Mary, lingering on Charlotte's blushing face.

'Because Charlotte lost her bag?' queried Alice in a high voice.

'No, silly. Because they are to be wed. Of course you know that or you wouldn't be here. Of course you've forgiven your parents their silly wish.'

'Oh no. You must be mistaken. He wouldn't ...'

A draught swept over Charlotte, someone had opened a door and let in the cold night air and the dark with it. Candles flickered. Aunt Mary's smile shrank to a grimace, she had fathomed out that Alice hadn't known, that they whispered secrets. And now Charlotte had to face Alice.

'It's not Charlotte's fault,' Nicholas burst out and stood up. 'She had no idea of our childish promise.'

But Charlotte knew now. The shock made the room swirl. She had suspected it of course but that's all it had been. And Nicholas had been lying and deceiving them both. She couldn't speak. She couldn't find her small voice. All she could do was rise and make haste to the door. Let the hallway lead to home, jaw clamped, black shawl around her, comfort in her old boots. Let her toss the jewels back in the sea where they belonged, for without them she would never have had fancy ideas, never have had ideas above her station, none of this would have happened.

And his Aunt Mary? Just biding her time, waiting to strike like a fat snake. Why hadn't she seen that spiteful deceitful look in the tilt of the old woman's head? The way she edged around the tables and chairs, the songs she sang on the piano? She must think Charlotte was some terrible girl, perhaps even a gold-digger. Charlotte was so far from home she suddenly missed the comfort her mother rocking by the fireside. She must gather her and Will's things and be gone from this house forever. They'd catch a carriage from the stable and go to King's Cross Station. Get the night train back home. The jewels would travel with her, once home she'd tie them to a rock and take them out on a boat once and for all and toss them where her mother had meant them to fall.

Chapter Sixteen

Nicholas thought Alice would never stop wailing and sobbing. He was flabbergasted by her reaction. He thought he knew her, not the unreasonable creature before him. Perhaps it was an act for the others. He uttered, 'But—' several times. She made all the sounds of having a broken heart.

His aunt looked on with amusement.

His ear lobes stung.

He gathered he'd been deceitful to both ladies.

To Alice mostly. And Charlotte hadn't even unwrapped the gift of the first edition romantic novel they'd discussed on his boat.

'But—'

When Alice had calmed down, he said he was 'sorry' and made other passive noises, he really meant it.

'But—' he tried again and was silenced by more hysteria.

He tried to catch the eye of Mrs Johnson to rescue him, but she was having none of it. They were all on Alice's side now.

Finally enough was enough and he shouted,

'BUT YOU DON'T LOVE ME, ALICE, YOU LOVE SOMEONE ELSE!'

There was as strange light in the room – an orange glow from the fire as the coals pulsed. He was stepping into deep waters, trespassing outside the realms of niceties.

Alice was taken aback.

'What?'

'I know. I've always known. You know I'm right. For goodness sake let me go and live my life instead of carrying on with this charade. Face up to the truth instead of fantasising what it might be like. Take a risk, Alice. Times are changing. What we do now is up to us. It's up to our generation to make changes for the better.

'You and I were never an item. Never made any promises to each other. Our parents did that and we just accepted it.

'We don't have to follow the course they mapped out for us. We haven't, we don't. We might have tried once but it never worked. Honestly in your heart and mind you know I'm right.'

'How dare you?'

He thought she would slap him but something was dawning on her, her rage was subsiding.

'I'm right aren't I?'

'You self-conceited righteous man. You are right! You are right.' She swung around, hands on her hips to the horrified onlookers.

'Well, what if he is right?' She moved to the fireplace and looked into its embers.

'I confess I'm in unknown territory now,' she said.

'It was a question of when one of us would say it, when one of us would do something about it.'

'I know you're right.'

'But, Nicholas,' Aunt Mary started up.

'It's none of your business.' He stared at his aunt with a cold heart.

'My dear,' said, Minnie to no-one in particular. 'I've got such a headache. Can I go home now?'

'I'll make some tea,' said Mrs Johnson.

And they waited for some steadiness to restore the space and crackles, they drank their tea in silence trying to fathom the revelations that they had hidden from each other, sighing in the relief.

Nicholas went to knock on Charlotte's door. He needed to speak to her urgently. He called her name.

She wasn't there. She wasn't in the house.

She'd taken Will with her.

Silly girl, he thought. But he had an ache as he stood outside in the dark street calling her name. A sudden chill ran right through him as if he had misplaced the most precious thing in the world.

Henry had more than one purse on his strings; little leather bags with leather laces that pulled tight. He had one inside each trouser pocket, and one in each of the inside pockets of his oilskin coat. He'd taken the trouble to sew several stitches of twine and knotted it through holes so he couldn't be parted from these bags easily. This was half the gold sovereigns he had left, the others were hidden under the floorboards of his lodgings. They were a real comfort to him on sleepless nights.

He looked up from the straw bale to the bridles, reigns and saddles and wondered why he had never taken to horses for a career, he was a natural. This horse that needed resting-up had led him here and he'd made an arrangement to rest with the horse for tonight. The stable lad didn't take any notice of a man lying there pondering.

Henry had woken from dozing and pieced together the match-seller girl winking at the mudlark and how they'd connived together and preyed on peoples' good natures. But he didn't mind that sort of canniness because the young ones needed food.

He also pieced together Charlotte's situation, well some of it. It was all down to that Captain O'Rourke. Aye. The man he'd trusted. He'd even let him in as a lodger and he'd gone and taken advantage of the girl. He must have lured her to London. Aye. To woo her. There weren't any long lost sovereigns, it was all in his imagination. He'd have found them by now or Sally would have revealed them by a look or a word. She was loyal and she cared for her babies. And the girl, well, she'd been just a kid – a young kid when her father went under. She would have sold or used any sovereigns they had long ago to keep them warm and feed them. Aye. It was Captain O'Rourke that had led her astray. It all made sense now. The man wi' 'is tales and 'is fancy words, he'd wooed her away to what? Marry her? He doubted it. He'd seen the shifty look in his Aunt Mary's eyes. Something weren't right. Aye. He'd have to hang around and keep an eye on how things progress, and if he had the chance he'd take the children back to Cromer and Sally. Keep them all safe. No more threats.

How could he have thought the girl was tricking him? She'd 'ad her 'ead turned. She was that age when they did. It was as if the horse, the preacher and the mudlark were all connected. Perhaps it was 'is mother's spirit. '*You make me proud, Henry, lookin' after the little ones,*' she'd have said.

His horse gave a soft whinny.

'Steady boy,' he said quietly.

And then the stable door burst open. Charlotte and Will stood there all flummoxed. The girl was a deathly white colour. And where was all her finery? All her new clothes? They both wore their old oilskin coats and the girl was wearing a pair of man's trousers by the looks of things. Will clutched a brown paper bag, books maybe.

'Yer 'ant been thieving 'ave yer?'

'Henry. Oh thank goodness, Henry. Please take us home,' said Charlotte, before she burst into tears.

Charlotte was mulling over events sitting on the edge of a hammock rocking with the motion of the schooner Henry had bundled them onto after doing some sort of a deal with the captain of the vessel. She pulled a prickly grey blanket over Will, though she doubted he would sleep, given the circumstances. Four sailors snoring, one Henry feigning sleep, two wide eyes questioning and a smell of sweaty men, damp linen and burning oil from the lanterns.

'What if the lantern falls over and sets fire to something?' asked Will.

'Oh Will, you know it won't happen,' she replied.

'It might.'

'You know these things have a way of going out if they fall over.'

'Do they?'

Charlotte wasn't really sure, she thought she had heard it said somewhere and had always just believed it.

'Tomorrow, we'll try it,' she suggested.

'Like an experiment?'

'Yes.' She couldn't ask Nicholas the question now, though she could ask Henry.

'Is it oak?'

'What?'

'The boat, silly. Oak's heavy isn't it. Yet it floats when it's shaped and joined together. I shall study a plan of the boat. Then if we get shipwrecked I can make us a small boat from the larger one. It's important to know these things.

'Charlotte, I'm glad we picked our books and pencils up. I don't care about the clothes. But your clothes did look nice. The lady ones I mean.'

'I'm glad we're going home, Will. I don't know whatever drove us to come here in the first place. It's odd don't you think, that we both decided to leave at the same time for the same place?'

'I try not to think about it. We both nearly drowned.'

'Yes. If it hadn't been for Nicholas …'

'I can't sleep.'

'I've noticed.'

'The hammocks swinging a bit.'

'Yes.'

'I don't suppose you'll sleep much.'

'No, I expect I won't.'

'Not when you've left Nicolas behind.'

'It all happened so fast, Will. Going to the stable, finding Henry there as if it were meant to be.' And the horses had pulled the coach to the docks urgently. She had cried in front of Henry for the first time. Thank goodness he hadn't hugged her or anything. He'd been brisk and thoughtful and soon had them in a coach hurrying to the docks. She'd huddled against the carriage in the sailor's clothes and oilskins.

'It'll be all right, Charlotte,' Will said now. 'I only wish I'd got to some of the places on my list of things to go and see and draw.'

'It was a long list. We'll come to London again and visit all the places together, when all this is settled.'

'That's something to look forward to. I wonder if I'll ever see Alice again.'

'Oh, Will.' She put her face close to his and lay down beside him on the hammock.

'Char, I have something to tell you. I sort of knew about Alice and Nicholas. I'm sorry I didn't tell you. I thought you were pretending like you said you were.'

'Oh, Will. Maybe I was pretending. Maybe we both were. I never meant to hurt Alice. I never meant to fall for Nicholas.'

'I know. It's all my fault.'

239

'No. Remember I was leaving too. I had some strange notions.'

'Do you really trust, Henry?' Will whispered.

Back in the stables she had been quick to believe Henry when he had told her he was innocent of any wrong doing and that he had been 'scaremongering' to stop Will blabbing because of the smuggling.

'He's done right by us, and if you think about it he always has. I guess everyone's entitled to make a mistake, let's hope that it's over and done with now,' she whispered. 'There's nothing he can do to us here anyway, not with all these other men about, you can sleep for a bit.'

'I shan't sleep. You've had a rubbish birthday haven't you?'

'Memorable I'd say.'

They fell silent, and Will closed his eyes. She imagined they were on a night train home, wondered what it was like speeding gently through the night, maybe a glimpse of the sea by the light of the moon, the cry of gulls, church bells silent. Instead there was all the rocking and swaying, strange men's snoring and coughing, the wind outside howling, the wild sea tossing the boat. She should never have left their mother alone. All three of her mother's carers were here on this boat. Oh please, let mother be all right. She should have left a footnote on the list she left for her mother:

I am sorry, Mother, I am young and foolish; I am greedy and I don't know why; something is inside me – a yearning – for what, I am not sure. The city was calling me, tempting me.

Perhaps fate played a hand luring me to save Will. When she saw her mother she would say:

Mother, I saved Will's life. Yes. This adventure was a response to save Will's life. Instinct central to everything. But I would ask you to think on this, Mother. To tell me what went on in that house in London. Did you steal, Mother? Riches and a baby? Did you steal me? And do you always trust Henry? We children find it hard to understand what he talks about? But you let him in and how many days and nights of not only summer but winter, mostly winter nights, has Henry sat by our fireside, puffing on his pipe, you rocking in your chair and the click, click of your needles. Will and I, taking care of each other. Perhaps things happen for a reason. All will be well, Mother. All will be well.

And then there was Alice. Now, she owed Alice an apology. Nicholas had betrayed Alice far more than he had her. Why ever did she carry on with the charade? She would write Alice a letter:

Dear, Sweet Alice,
No,
My Dearest Alice,
No,
Dearest Alice,
Or,
Dear Alice,
I'm so sorry for what happened. I'm sorry for everything. I want you to know that Nicholas and I

were never anything more than friends, I'm not even sure we were that – more acquaintances. You should know that he was acting to protect Will from Henry, whom we both believed (as you know) to be a bad man. Henry has shown himself to be acting on nothing more than foolishness which was wrongly interpreted by us as a wish to harm Will. In fact, nothing could be further from the truth. I was convinced I had to protect Will and we found ourselves at the mercy of 'The Devil's Throat'. It was Nicholas that saved us both from drowning. Nicholas showed us both nothing but kindness and for that I am most grateful.

I'm afraid the fault lies with me, I may have had a girlish crush on Nicholas and he went along with my lies and deceit to protect us. The fault is all mine. Perhaps it was my youth and naivety. Please forgive me.

Dear Sweet Alice. I am all to blame.

Yours Charlotte.

And to Nicolas she would write; no, she hadn't finished her letter to Alice, she would put a footnote.

Alice, think on this, why would Nicholas come up with the preposterous idea in the first place? Why did he kiss me? Why did he look into my eyes and hold that gaze of his? Why did he breathe hard when he crushed me to him? Why did he hold my hand like he did?

Does he really love you, Alice? Can you honestly spend your life with a man that can do these things with another? Can you, Alice? Can you?

She wiped her the tears dripping from her nose on the sleeve of her gansey, careful not to disturb Will, he was sleeping, and she wondered if this was what it was like to be a mother to a child. Poor Will, she kissed his forehead.

Close by, Henry was swinging back and forth in a hammock. Back and forth like her belief in him, and if she was honest she wanted to believe he was telling the truth. Was Will being persuaded by Henry, saying that on that terrible night, Will had exaggerated, so that poor Henry was being accused of something that could see him hanged? Was Henry resorting to his wits to maintain his innocence?

Now, they were trapped with him on a boat heading out to sea. Charlotte shivered. She would try and stay awake to watch over Will.

Sally was watching the woman they force-fed in the next bed, her bony hands and fingers twisted and turned, plaiting long grey hair. Lamplight flickered in the room as if a gust of wind blew them; the other women noticed it too, some stopped brushing their hair, and some sat up putting their hands on their heads or over their eyes. Just because they can, thought Sally, wondering if the mad woman's ranting earlier meant anything, would something happen in the dark? Did they all know something she didn't?

There was a noise outside, she imagined if what she could hear might be a man in a heavy coat and balaclava, stooped over the frozen ground, he chopped into the barren earth with a spade, chop, chop, he went. Perhaps he was getting paid to dig by a lone lamplight he placed on the ground near him. As he never moved any earth does he belong here, on another ward? Was there a man's ward? Should she fear the cut of the blade, or was he there for exercise? In the tiny distant window she saw a flurry of snow.

She wondered what the chances were of the ward door being locked, she eyed it hungrily but she was filled with apathy and couldn't muster the energy to go and find out, besides the floorboards were not solid, they swayed and lurched and she doubted she would be able to keep her balance, which would mean she'd have to crawl but that might look a bit strange and make her stand out from these other women. Never mind, so be it, she slipped her legs from under the sheets and blankets but as much as she willed her legs they stayed still. She wasn't tied down, all she had to do was run, just run. She tried to scream 'RUN', but nothing came out of her mouth. She drew in a deep breath of cold air and realised it was the dose holding her back. What was the matter with everyone else? Why don't they run? Why are they tied up sometimes and not others?

She let out a long loud wail, followed by – 'It's her birthday. I've missed her birthday again.' It was too much, she always let Charlotte down, and she curled over and heaved great sobs.

'All this self-pity.' The bird orderly fluttered down from the ceiling. 'It won't do. It just won't do.'

And there was some relief in the sweet liquid she poured down her throat. Sally realised she didn't want another dose, it was too soon after the last one. She lifted her arms and tried to knock the dose away. A sharp sting slapped her on her face. She fell back instantly, and then there were other hands and she was being tied down.

'Help me. O help me,' she cried.

Nicholas strode with purpose, the docks stretched out in front of him, and he meant to walk every blessed mile of it and search every ship and boat to find her. *How many is that?* someone might ask. And he'd reply, perhaps a thousand or two, or five thousand or many more. There was a hum even at this hour between the masts of the vessels, some were clanking here and there, flags fluttered lightly though it was hard to see them, and the mist was slowly rising as the breeze subsided. It had snowed earlier but it had been little more than a flurry, for that he was glad.

'How much, mister?' cried a sack-maker, from a group of five sewing under the lamplight.

'Not tonight,' he replied gruffly, though he knew she was only teasing. She went back to her stitching, leaning on the post with a sigh.

Nicholas stopped walking and turned around.

'Have you seen a girl, she'd be dressed like a boy, long black hair, perhaps plaited and hanging down the front side, she'd have a boy with her, about ten years old?' It was about the hundredth time he'd asked this night, and he'd almost given up on asking again.

There was some whispering among them until the woman held out her palm. He pulled out a shilling from his pocket.

'They went to the Jolly Tar, mister,' she nodded in the direction. He was doubly fortunate, there were so many Jolly Tar's.

'If you're looking for them, it were ages ago. They were looking for a ride home. There was a man wi' em.'

'What did he look like?'

She described Henry.

'Thank you. Thank you.'

There was no gold in the streets tonight, there was yellow sou'westers and hunched over men, there was grey in the women sack-makers, grey in the shadows of the ladies of the night, and the men wandering between them and the ale houses. The vessels in this light were all grey, and so were the dolphins that that wrapped around the lantern posts along the river that would never leave their warm posts, their eyes flickered yellow in the light, and perhaps their skin glinted silver.

What was Charlotte thinking? What did he know about her really? Perhaps it was after all just that he hadn't been with a woman in a long time and she was so damn attractive.

The silly girl had left without even waiting for an explanation.

She thought him dishonest.

Perhaps he had previously been content with the arrangement with Alice. It meant he had avoided anything to do with commitment to anyone else.

And Charlotte had changed all that.

'Mr O'Rourke?'

Nicholas, a little surprised by the man's voice, he turned to a carriage which stopped beside him.

'Aye,' he replied.

'It's me. I was the doctor at your house.'

'Ah, yes.'

The man was leaning out of the carriage window now.

'I've just come from a job,' he said as if reading Nicholas's mind. 'Would you believe some drunk captain walked a plank which gave way and he fell into the sea, got caught up in chains and banged his head on an anchor?'

'Aye, I would believe it,' Nicholas chuckled.

'Can I give you a lift, Captain O'Rourke?'

'I'm looking for someone. I have a lead, I have to check at this inn.'

'I have something urgent to share with you, Mr O'Rourke. I fear their may have been some wrong-doing. I'd really like your opinion on the matter.'

He sounded so earnest Nicholas said, 'Could you wait five minutes? I have to make this enquiry first.'

'Of course.' The doctor closed the window and sat back.

Chapter Seventeen

Charlotte gasped as a jolt tossed her from the hammock. She had been dreaming of falling down a deep dark well. She was aware she was in a nightmare and her mind was in two places at once, until she hit the floor.

'Charlotte, are you all right?'

Even though it was pitch black she knew the hammock that was swinging over her head had Will clinging on to it. The boat was groaning as it were straining not to tip up and spill all its contents into the sea and not to break apart.

Henry was cursing. Several sailors were scrambling up the ladder to the deck.

They had to get out. She could smell kerosene. The lamps had tipped up.

'Will? Charlotte?' Henry was beside them.

'Here,' she shouted.

She was glad of him, for his strength. He put his arms under her and dragged her to her feet while steadying the hammock for Will to clamber out.

She could hear a crackling and a sudden flicker of flame started up in a far corner.

'Come on,' shouted Henry, as the flicker turned into a blaze.

Her eyes quickly adjusted in the light of the blaze, she could see a trickle of sweat on Henry's brow. Somehow he picked Will up under one arm and dipping and weaving he dragged her to the ladder.

She could hardly move but knew she had to be quick. Moments later she was on the deck. Rain lashed her with icy belts, the wind threw her off balance. The boat lurched again.

'Charlotte, grab Will!' shouted Henry from below.

'Listen, Will. Listen. Grab my hands,' she yelled.

And it was Henry's strength that shoved Will up the ladder, and she clung to Will and dragged him upon the deck. And Henry followed with keen eyes and hidden strength, and she could hear him roaring to locate the other men. She could hear flames swallowing the hammocks beneath her along with their books and pencils.

Henry gathered Will to him under one arm and pulled her by her wrist.

'They left us!' she bellowed.

'Nothing shall harm yee on my watch,' shouted Henry.

Charlotte's eyes brimmed over with tears. How could she have misjudged the man so much?

Something snapped.

The mast! Henry pulled her along by her wrist. Some of the men were running, they were like dark shadows in the pelting rain, slipping and sliding on the wet deck. She knew then they were all making for the lifeboats.

She heard boom and the sound of a missile whirring through the storm.

They weren't far from shore then?

Henry was pulling them towards a lifeboat. He was shouting something at a raggedy man climbing into the craft. One of the men seated stood up and fired a pistol.

'No more room. Go to the other boat! The man yelled.

'For God's sake man, they're just children,' Henry roared back.

The wind whipped through the sails and a moment later the man with the pistol shouted, 'Take the oar, man.'

Henry didn't pause, he pulled Will and her and somehow wedged them between two soaked men and took his place as the boat was lowered over the side.

Will was shivering, she hugged him tight.

Henry began shouting commands, he knew the treacherous sea; he trained with the lifeboat men. He turned the little craft and guided it over the crashing waves. Henry, whom she had thought was going to murder Will. Henry whom they'd fled from. Henry whom they believed was stalking them and chasing them with murder on his mind.

How foolish she was. How naïve. How utterly, utterly childish.

'There's land ahoy!' he yelled reassuringly. 'Almost there!'

Henry manoeuvred the light craft so the high waves lifted and carried them rapidly to the shore, where men and women were running with blankets and waving lanterns all along the beach. Charlotte was overwhelmed with gratitude towards them, and she realised, to Henry.

Sally wondered if she would ever see beyond her husband's death. She had become a wretched wreck unable to sleep at night. The constant ebbing and flowing of the tides revealed nothing of him. Longshore drift did not carry him to any golden sand bank. Perhaps he headed for one of the Scandinavian countries or the artic. Perhaps he swam with whales.

She remembered how she went looking for him once, took a rowing boat out to sea. The vastness of the sea startled her, she rowed to a horizon she would never reach, and she bobbed on the North Sea like she was nothing. Henry had found her. He rescued her and brought her back, shivering, hungry, and wide-eyed. She remembered him talking gently. She remembered him gathering her up with all the pieces of her broken heart. But he couldn't fix the pieces of her heart back together. She wished Henry was here now as she lay in the dark. The man outside had stopped chopping but she listened carefully, there was some terrible ice-walker on the ward. Someone was chanting a prayer under a blanket. Someone was whispering, *no, no*.

She was not safe.

'Clara, Clara, is that you?'

'Don't be afraid. It will soon be over,' Clara replied.

And then there was lantern-light flooding the ward along with three ward orderlies. And the women were being pulled from their beds and told to walk. They filed obediently one behind the other. In bare feet they huddled and shuffled along. They were sorry looking souls. She wasn't shackled to the bed anymore but she waited numbly until it was her turn as it seemed the best thing to do. To join in, to get in line and shuffle along by lantern-light.

'You won't tell anyone will you?' the woman behind her asked.

No one answered her.

Sally thought if she had died at sea, her children would have been orphans.

Henry said she had to give it time to get over John. Where had time gone? She had a lot of memories of time. And images of the sea and the beach. Sand time, then.

The orderlies were men

She wasn't safe.

Yet all the women shuffled along. They were going down a dark corridor.

'Is it sand time?' she shouted.

No one answered.

They were going down some steep concrete steps, she held on to a thick rope and inched down with the others. She'd held rope like this before. The rope of wrecks. Lost ropes. Frayed ropes. Abandoned ropes.

There was flickering light.

There was a wall and they all shuffled to it. She could see fear in the women's wide eyes, hear it in the cries. Clara took her hand.

'It's all right. It'll soon be over. It's another one of the doctor's experiments.'

She wasn't safe.

The floor was writhing.

'It's just the drugs they give you,' said Clara. 'Brace yourself. It's only water.'

And then it came from wide-mouthed hosepipes the orderlies were aiming at them. The ice-cold water flooded in. Pushing, shoving, and gushing. Torrents of it against her body. Her head hit the wall. And her legs gave way.

Clara, she knew it was Clara as weak as she was kept a tight grip of her hand. Clara meant to stop her from drowning.

Someone was screaming. She didn't have the strength. She just had to breathe. Gasp between the torrents.

'Think of your children!' Clara yelled.

She thought of Will. Her baby. She cradled him seconds after he was born, oh the scent of him and his cry.

And the water stopped. And she hadn't drowned. Not this time anyway. And the ground floor was covered in water, it ran and glugged to a drain. And there was naked feet and melancholy women in wet nighties and drenched hair and some were suffering from hysteria. And they were being shuffled again. She had Clara's hand and Clara was leaning over coughing up blood which splattered onto the water and the blood began to spread and run down with the water to the drain.

Chapter Eighteen

'I threw the stone down, lad, and a stone lands where it lands and it takes something or someone to move it. Sometimes it's a heavy stone to shift, by then it's a rock. But you know some stones roll and some bounce but the big rock, aye, it might take a heavy sea to shift it. Will, lad, I never meant to throw a rock or stone at yee. Yew 'ave a sensitive nature, aye, that you dew, lad, that you dew.'

Will looked at Charlotte. He wanted to ask her what Henry was talking about but his teeth were chattering and there was so much commotion on the beach, plus the wind and rain, and he could hardly ask the question when Henry was stood there, but then he realised he got the gist of what Henry said, Henry was apologising for scaring him.

'Aye, the villagers and their lanterns. There's the lifeboat crew out there in them treacherous waves. Are we all accounted for?' Henry looked around.

Another rocket flare whizzed across the waves and reached the stricken vessel. Will could make out the lifeboat men had reached the other sailors in the boat still being thrown about at sea. The lifeboat men fastened the small craft to a rope, and soon they were in wading distance of the beach.

'All safe then,' said Henry.

Will clung to Charlotte's hand, someone replaced the soaked through blanket with a dry one and she pulled it around them both.

'Shall we bag ourselves a few oranges?' asked Henry.

The beach was littered with little spots of orange on the dark beach, and they fell and rolled on the strand line. The rain stopped, the sea swell subsided as fast as it had risen, and Will noticed more and more blobs of orange.

'Bug buggers aren't they?' said Henry.

'Make your pockets bulge,' Charlotte said.

Will laughed shakily. 'I knew I could smell oranges,' he said, bending over to retrieve one that rolled to his feet.

They were led away by a kindly lady and they found themselves sitting in an alehouse by a crackling fire. Someone began serving out brandy, Will didn't want the stuff, and he gave his to Henry. Henry asked for hot tea for 'the young un's'. Will looked closely at his sister, Charlotte's face was white, her black hair was falling out of its plait and around her forehead it began to make wispy curls.

'We've been in worse,' she said, squeezing his hand over the table.

'They want to give a bed for the rest of the night,' said Henry. 'I don't know about you but I want to get home. I've had enough of this malarkey.'

'Me too,' said Will.

'Aye, and me,' said Charlotte. The jewels were heavy stones around her neck and deep in her pockets. Heavy stones between the wretched wreck and the dinging bells.

'It's freezing,' said Will. He hugged his arms around his new sweater as the carriage stopped outside Cromer church.

'There's no smoke from the chimney,' said Henry, peering out of the small carriage window.

'The bells are silent at least,' remarked Charlotte.

As they got out Will noticed a gull peering down at them from the head of a gargoyle. 'The ghost of a bird,' he said.

'What?' asked Henry.

'Nothing,' replied Will.

'We smell of oranges now,' said Charlotte.

'Aye,' chuckled Henry.

Will watched Henry effortlessly throw a sack of oranges over his shoulder. He thought back to how Henry had disappeared for several minutes at the alehouse and returned with clean dry clothes for them, along with the sack of oranges and a carriage booked,. He had a knack of making things appear, and now, Will picked up the sack of their damp clothes and thought the new trousers and knitted sweater he wore were much more comfortable than any of the new stuff he'd left behind at Summerville House and with Peter.

I'm glad to be home, he thought. He'd find some bread for the gull, and later go to the school house and tell the mistress he'd been ill for a few days and all would be well. Perhaps he'd tell his friends about his real adventures.

'Do you think I'll ever see Peter again? Could I write to him? Can he read? Could he come to stay with us?

'So many questions,' replied Charlotte. 'Let's see our mother first. Let's get some sleep, then we'll talk about Peter.'

The carriage drew away pulled by tired looking bay mares.

'London seems so far away already,' he said.

'Yes, that it does, Will, that it does,' said Charlotte wistfully.

'I think I'd like to write down of our adventures,' said Will. 'The things we saw and the people we met.'

Henry looked at him sternly.

'Perhaps not,' he said.

Henry winked. He had acquired an Aran cabled sweater and black trousers, Will thought the look suited him, it was warm looking. He didn't wholly trust Henry, but Henry had proved himself, he'd saved their lives. When Henry had gone off in the alehouse, Charlotte had told him that Henry was a complicated man. Henry was that all right. The man stood looking down the alley at their cottage and took off his cap and slapped his thigh with it.

Will would beat Henry to his back door. He'd never wanted to get home more in his life. He hoped his mother was lucid. Still taking the watered down dose Charlotte had been giving her. He knew all about it. You couldn't live with someone and be cared for by them without knowing something of what they were doing.

He took the spare key from underneath a flint rock by the door. He ran through the rooms of the cottage, the rooms were cold and empty.

They opened and closed doors. Oranges spilled onto the kitchen table. Henry disappeared 'to make enquiries'. Charlotte stood by the grey ashes of the fire, Will knew she was thinking the worst about their mother. He could see his sister's hands tremble as she shuffled ashes with a poker; she got on her knees and began to shovel them into a bucket.

'She wouldn't Charlotte. She just wouldn't do anything stupid.'

Moments later Will sensed Henry behind them, he had a familiar tobacco smell and now it mingled with a woolly sweater one.

'Now then. I tell you Sally has buckled up. She's as solid as an oak table now. Moose goose, she's all up and taken to riding on trains and chuffed it up to fancy herself as mother-of-the-bride.'

'She's gone to London?' said Charlotte, surprised and relieved at the same time.

'Yes. She's gone to look for you children.'

'What shall we do?' asked Will.

'I'll get the next train up and bring her home,' said Henry.

'Oh, Henry,' said Charlotte.

'I'll sleep on the train,' he said. You two rest up, get the fire on, and get a stew on. I'll be back with your mother in a day.'

'But what if you pass her on the train on her way back when she finds us gone?'

'Nay, lass, don't worry. I'll just get the train back again, and will have had a good sleep to catch up on.'

Charlotte sat down in the chair beside the cold ashes. She found the crumpled list of 'things to do' she had left for her mother. She got on her knees again and shuffled the last of the ashes in the cold grate and put the crumpled paper back with a few sticks of wood around it to get a fire going.

'How on earth can she find her way around London on her own?'

'Lass. It's surprising what you can do – even in dreams. She'll be at Summerville House, and I'll have some explaining to do to that captain of yours, and he to me.'

Charlotte and Will looked up in surprise.

'You will be all right while I'm gone?' asked Henry.

'Of course. I'm used to taking care of us,' she answered.

'Things that 'appen, they can make or break you. That's the long and the short of it. Take the path down to the beach, watch for sails on the horizon, it's surprising what the winds will bring.'

'What are you trying to say, Henry?'

'It's just a day away and I'll bring back your mother. The speed of it – the train. And the horses and carriages, why they'll have to be quick. You have unfinished business with your captain.'

'No. My business with that man is finished.'

261

Will could see Charlotte hunching over the fire. He went over to her and put a hand on her shoulder.

'I'll do that,' he said.

Nicholas wondered if he'd made the right decision by not following Charlotte back to Cromer when he'd heard she and Will had sailed away with Henry. The schooner they'd boarded had been heading for Cromer with a cargo of oranges. But could Henry be trusted not to harm Will and Charlotte? Had Will and Henry sorted out what really happened the night of the wreck on the beach? He'd been at least an hour at the house after Charlotte had left. He must have been at least two or three hours looking for them both at the docks, another hour to get here, and then there was all the waiting around in wind and gales. He prayed to God the business with Henry had all been a misunderstanding and he was doing the right thing now. He'd go to the train station as soon as he was out of here. It was already morning. He looked around at the entrance hall to the asylum. It had a long wide room with a highly polished wooden floor, the floor reflected the morning's low light, and it streamed in the door and windows giving the floor a sheen like a calm sea. On the floor both side of the walls were single occupancy chairs, and the walls had sets of curtains that could section off the hallway into little rooms for privacy. Dr Pope and he, edged cautiously for the opposite door to which that they had entered, although they had been told to wait by an orderly.

'Dr Farish!'

'Dr Pope,' the other doctor replied, holding out his hand for a firm handshake, and then looking curiously at Nicholas.

'And you are?' Dr Farish had to look up to meet Nicholas's intense stare.

'Captain O'Rourke.'

The doctor looked up to the left side of the ceiling. Nicholas guessed he was trying to place him, perhaps he had been mentioned in part of Sally's story …

'How can I help you gentlemen?' Dr Farish took out his pocket watch from his top jacket pocket and flipped the cover, he glanced at the timepiece as if they were keeping him from something.

'May we step inside your office,' said Dr Pope.

'Regarding?'

'A patient of yours. Sally Mayhew.'

'Sally Mayhew?'

'Yes. Captain O'Rourke is her prospective son-in-law.'

'What?'

'Yes, Dr Farish. You heard correctly,' said Nicholas.

'Gentlemen, would you like to step into my office? Some tea perhaps?' He clicked his fingers at an orderly who stood close behind him.

Sally recalled how she had dried herself down with a grey towel and had obediently got into a dry nightie. She had wanted to sit on Clara's bed and watch and listen to her. She wasn't sure Clara was mad at all but she did wonder about the poor woman's breathing which she had listened too for what seemed like hours until it suddenly went quiet. Only a few days ago she had been watching over Will. Oh, but the young had a way of bouncing back. Clara was all bone and haunches, white hair and purple bruises.

'Clara?'

Sally moved her arms freely, she wasn't tied down. She swung her legs out of the bed, it was easy now she had stopped shaking and the floor had stopped writhing.

She was sure the sun was up, an orderly sat at a desk the other end of the room with his head on his arms, flat out asleep.

No one to see me, she thought. So like a shadow I'll stand beside Clara and hold her hand and say thank you.

Clara's hand was cold. Clara's fingers were stiff.

Morning light strained through the small round window.

'You can go home now, Clara,' she whispered. Where did she live? Did she have family?

She closed Clara's eyes.

Sally heard far away voices turning into figures with grey shadows. One of them had a familiar stance. Tall. Distinguished.

A visitor for her?

'Mrs Mayhew?' he said. 'Sally? It's Captain O'Rourke. Charlotte's betrothed. I've come to take you home,' he said.

'Clara's dead,' said Sally. 'Look what they've done. My friend is dead. She wasn't melancholy. Look how thin she is. She how she bled from her mouth. How her stomach is distended, how easily she bruised.'

'She's with God now,' said the kindly looking man standing next to the captain.

'It's her condition. That's all,' said Dr Farish defensively.

'No sea-bed for Clara,' said Sally. 'A nice spot under a beech tree where the bells ring on a Sunday. Shall you see to it Dr Farish? If she has no kin send me the bill. If you do that we'll say no more on the matter. I'll be on my way now.'

Sally was aware of quickly pulling on the clothes she had arrived in. Then taking the arm of Dr Pope who had escorted Captain O'Rourke, and he also insisted she take his arm. She glided across a sea of a floor to the outside and into a carriage.

Only then did she let out a sob, and then another, only when the carriage pulled away did she fall forwards and let the tears fall.

'You've had a lucky escape there, Mrs Mayhew,' said Dr Pope.

'Yes,' she whispered. And then she found herself telling her rescuers, 'I loved him you know. John. My John. Never mind her, Kathryn, Alice's mother. John loved me in the end. I know he did.'

'What are you saying, Sally?' Nicholas asked.

'He loved me, we grew to love each other, and I was prepared to give everything up to raise his daughter as my own. Love her as I would my own child.'

'Are you saying Charlotte isn't your birth daughter?'

'Charlotte was Kathryn Merryweather's daughter. She gave her up.' There it was out. A heavy weight fell into the sea, and she'd plunged into a deep dark shadow and surfaced again.

'What happened?' asked Nicholas.

He had a right to know if he going to wed her. He might not like what she is. He might go away and never come back and Charlotte would never have to marry a sailor. If he didn't go away then he must truly love her, let it be his decision.

'Kathryn had a brief fling with my husband, before he was my husband. Whilst she was on holiday. I was there, or thereabouts looking after her other children, James and Alice. Alice was just a baby then. It could not have been Mr Merryweather's child you see because he had been abroad for six months and no matter how she tried to fix it, the dates could not lie. Fate played a hand because John saved his life and when he came to London for his reward at their London house the baby had not long been born. They were all set to take the baby to the orphanage because Kathryn's husband wouldn't accept the baby as his own. Kathryn pleaded with her husband and it was agreed I would take the child and raise her. And John was convinced to marry me for a large sum of gold sovereigns, and we would raise the child together. Kathryn's husband never knew John was the real father.

'As I got into the carriage that would take us away a large trunk of baby things was given. When we unpacked I found lots of jewels and a note from Kathryn, the note said: *For my baby girl, should you ever fall on hard times. Love forever, Mother.*

'I'm not sure John ever understood any of it, he was thrown into the situation as quickly as I was. But we couldn't let Charlotte go to an orphanage. I'm sure John grew to love me. Sometimes the sun would shine all day on our cottage. Charlotte was truly loved.'

'And Charlotte, she's never known the truth about her real mother?'

'No. Sally shook her head. 'John and I argued so much about whether to tell her. Many times I nearly sold the jewels and took her and Will to live by ourselves. Many times I asked John where he kept the gold he had left over after he'd brought the cottage and his own boat. I fear it was stolen from his boat after he fell overboard. Or was he killed for it and his body got rid of? I'll never know.'

'Right now we have to get the next train back to Cromer. Are you well enough to travel? Dr Pope, is Sally well enough to travel?'

'Well I would recommend rest. But you can rest on the train and at home. We'll find out when the next train is due, if it's this afternoon you can both rest at my house until then. Our house is not too far from the station.'

At the train station while Nicholas checked the departures he heard a newspaper seller shouting, 'Another schooner sinks off the Norfolk Coast!'

He purchased a paper and scanned the headlines. As he read he learned there were no casualties, no deaths. And he had to lean on a post to regain his composure. He decided to keep the news from Sally for now. Let the woman rest a little at Dr Pope's house for there was no train to Cromer until the afternoon.

Charlotte stood a little way inside the door of The Shed in her men's trousers and her old gansey with a sense of theatre, she placed a hand on her hip, and occasionally lifted up and dropped her plaited hair. Since her arrival, Will had attached himself to a boy his own age and they raced crabs on the floor. Will seemed recovered from his ordeals 'but', she explained to her friend 'they were searching for their mother'. Everyone knew of Sally's mood swings due to her addiction, and everyone had had dealings with Henry at some time or another. Charlotte knew this gave her an advantage over many of the other workers who would have been told not to come back, and although Charlotte never wanted to come back she needed to know she could if it was necessary.

She called Will and they walked down to the beach. A few folk were still scrambling for any wreckage they could salvage. Charlotte watched her neighbours scavenging and wondered when she had begun to have ideas above her station. Had it been her mother – Sally's teachings, making her speak correctly, educating her with language and maths beyond what most of her friends could ever imagine. Weren't women still bound by marriage and status?

It was freezing cold and for a moment she wished for the warmth of the new cloak she had left behind in London.

It would most likely be at least a day before Henry returned with their mother. She couldn't get Alice's mother out of her head. She tried to piece Sally's part in the having possession of the jewels that had hung around Alice's mother's throat in the portrait. Should she return them to the sea were her mother had meant them to land. But her mother was hardly ever rational was she? There was change in the air, it ebbed and then swelled forward with more force than she could control, as if the tide were bringing them all back to her, Sally, Henry and Nicholas.

When the rain began to fall she called to Will and headed home. A man was approaching, she recognised him as one of the lifeboat men and fishermen. He looked earnest, a hat on his head rather like Henry's, and he lifted his hat on meeting her. He carried something navy blue in his other hand and he was holding it out as if to present her with it.

'The Dane's delivered it,' he said, as he stopped walking.

She could walk past him. The sky was darkening. The tide was rushing, turning, sloshing.

'Do you recognise the pattern?'

A stupid question because obviously she'd seen the pattern knitted and unravelled a thousand times by her mother.

'It was your father's.'

And she held her hands out to receive the scrap of rag, and she wanted to ask, was there any bones? Was there? Was there? But Will was standing quietly beside her and she took his hand and held it tight.

'Is that it? Is that all there is left of him?' she cried, startled by her own voice.

That afternoon at Dr Pope's house Sally woke up alarmed, she couldn't believe she'd dozed off. Perhaps she felt safe in this man's company. He was a handsome man what with his black pony-tail, the dimple in his chin and his piercing blue eyes, which were closed as if he slept soundly.

Sally heard the noise of horses and carriages outside in the road where Dr Pope and his wife lived. At that moment the door opened and Mrs Pope carried in a tray laden with tea things. Nicholas didn't stir and she put the tray down quietly on an elaborately carved tea-table.

Sally shivered. Mrs Pope must have noticed because she stoked the fire and when she replaced the poker she stood back and leaned on the mantelpiece. Sally thought the young woman was going to say something wise or clever, but she didn't speak and for that Sally was grateful.

All these people willing to help her now. She wished they'd been there when John had gone missing. But, she realised, Henry had been there, and so had Charlotte, young as she was. And how had she repaid them? All that time wasted floundering. Nothing was ever clear. The power of it – the laudanum and the grief. She hadn't planned any of it, she'd adapted instead. Had she done those years through self-pity? Did it matter now? She could do everything differently now she was moving and living again. But still she let Mrs Pope pass her a cup of tea because she feared she might spill the tea or drop the cups.

The two of them sat together on the sofa in comfortable silence so as not to wake Nicholas until Dr Pope's carriage returned to take them back to the train station.

When Sally thanked Mrs Pope she did so sincerely with the promise she would visit should she ever be in Cromer again.

In the carriage alone with Nicholas she listened to him tell the story of how he and Charlotte got together.

'… and the two of them boarded my boat. They had a crazy idea to go to London to sell the jewels. I thought Charlotte was older though I recognised Will from your cottage. I wasn't sure if what they had planned had anything to do with the smuggler on the beach. Perhaps they'd seen something, picked up the jewels and were being chased by other smugglers. I had to protect them until I found out the truth and so I went along with their story …'

Sally thought he wasn't being wholly truthful, some of what he said made sense though. Years ago she'd tossed those jewels into the sea, Charlotte must have seen her do it and gone into the sea to retrieve them. Now he was saying something about another woman.

'… and Alice. We went along with our parents' wishes but in reality we never believed we would ever be married. Though I think Alice did more than I.'

'Poor Alice.'

'No. Not poor Alice. Alice was – is in love with someone else. She is free now to be with him. But Charlotte fled when my aunt told her Alice and I were promised to each other. She fled taking Will with her. Somehow they got on a night boat to Cromer. Sally, the schooner came aground at Happisborough. But all is well, Sally. Everyone was taken ashore safely. Here.'

She took the newspaper being thrust at her and scanned the headlines.

'Good grief. You're sure they were in this boat?'

'I'm certain. And Henry was with them.'

'Henry?'

'Aye. Read on.'

And she did so. And then she said, 'It sounds like Henry is some kind of hero. He won't like that. He'd just be doing what any caring man would do in that situation.'

'It's a credit to him,' said Nicholas.

'Thank goodness he was there.'

'Aye. Maybe these things happen for a reason.'

Sally's mind was swirling with all these stories. She badly needed a swig of her laudanum, but dare not take one in front of this man.

'So you were engaged to the beautiful little Alice Merryweather?'

'Aye.'

'And you're the Nicholas O'Rourke that used to play with James when he was little.'

'Yes. We were always friends.'

'How is James?'

'He's a vicar now, down South, Brighton way.'

'He always was a gentle soul.'

'He still is.'

Sally smiled. 'I missed those children. But I did as I was told. Mr Merryweather said if we ever returned or made contact they'd have Charlotte taken away to an orphanage. He can't do that now can he? We can tell Charlotte everything?'

'Aye. We can,' said Nicholas.

Sally had a sudden view of the train station. All the horses and carriages arriving, leaving and standing still. People were walking and entering the grand gates of the station, or leaving them. There were coachmen in their tall hats and mackintoshes, train drivers and conductors in their shiny-buttoned uniforms, and amongst them, men and women with suitcases and shopping bags and children. A breeze carried the hum of clopping hooves and voices, a warm scent of life. And although it was a grey December day this was a snapshot she would remember; everyone going about their business knowing where they were going and where they had been and that was enough for this moment. It was marvellous to see even if it was from the edges.

And then she saw Henry! He was standing still hailing a carriage. He wore a white Aran sweater. Where had he got that from?

'It's Henry!' she cried.

'What?'

'Henry. Over there.'

Nicholas stopped the carriage, got out and ran towards Henry.

Sally watched them meet. Henry stood his ground as Nicholas slowed down approaching him – out of breath, one hand in his pocket.

Henry put out his hand in a friendly gesture and said something.

She prayed under her breath for Nicholas to take Henry's hand for she'd seen a grave look pass over Nicholas. There was more to this story than he was letting on. Perhaps the real story involved Henry in some way. The truth would out sometime. For now, she was more concerned to get home to her children. She rummaged in her bag to have a quick dose before anyone could see her. And then she'd go to Henry. He never let her down. She had missed him. How kind he was. How patient. How caring. How misunderstood. And when he approached the carriage, she thought, how handsome.

'My dearest,' she said, climbing down to greet him.

'Sally. Oh Sally. What yer doing 'ere?' Whatever's happened to yer?'

And she was embraced by his strong arms and allowed herself a little sob.

Chapter Nineteen

'Do you still have that book, Charlotte, *What Girls Can Do?*'

Charlotte smiled at her mother, Sally.

'You surpass all expectations,' her mother said. 'Travelling, knitting, reading, cooking, let alone the teaching at the school and writing a recipe book.'

'The teaching is only temporary, Mother. You know that, it's only until the new mistress arrives.'

'Well nevertheless. How's your book coming along?'

'Good. Will's becoming quite skilled at drawing, he can complement the recipes with detailed illustrations. He's fast becoming a talented artist under the supervision of Alice.'

Sally tossed a spray of bluebells on her husband's grave.

'He was quite partial to macaroons if I remember correctly. I'm not sure what he would make of 'Ways With Fish', said Charlotte.

'I think he'd approve very much indeed. Do you think he'd approve of what I'm doing? Am I betraying him?'

'No, Mother. Henry is all right. He has proved himself to be trustworthy over and over.' Charlotte turned to her mother.

'I've actually known Henry for much longer than you might realise,' said Sally. 'From years back in fact. I wasn't much older than you. When I was nanny for the Merryweathers's. I remember Henry in the market square in London. He whistled and slapped his cap on his leg and said: 'Morning.' I think I laughed coyly, then Kathryn Merryweather said, 'Come along, Sally, do not fraternise,' all haughty like.

'Then when you were about three years of age we were on the beach and I met him again, he'd come in on some boat or other and he whistled at me again. This time we talked a little. I told him I was married.

'I don't think he ever left Cromer for long after our second meeting. He said the town was a fine place to settle down. He said there was 'opportunities'. And you know there was many a morning when I'd catch him watching me long after I'd passed him. It's like he's always been there for me to fall back on. He's grown on me over the years. And he doesn't mind about the laudanum, he knows I'll never be able to stop it completely. Though I shall try with your help.

'Charlotte, I'm so proud of you. When I came home that day with Henry, and told you everything about Kathryn Merryweather, I'd thought I'd lose you forever.'

'I understood, it all made sense then, everything slotted into place, the jewels, the arguing, my education. I'm just glad you took me in and I wasn't left in an orphanage.'

'We did more than that. We loved you. I loved you. I love you like my own daughter. You are my child and always will be.

'And when Alice's letter came it wasn't such a shock was it? I think it was more of a shock for her,

277

especially her parent's attitude after what her mother had done. And she even explained about Nicholas and their parents' wishes which neither of them wanted to fulfil.'

Charlotte didn't want to dwell on this matter, it was all behind her now.

'You look beautiful, Mother.' Charlotte put back a wisp of hair in Sally's carefully pinned up locks. Sally wore a white muslin dress with prints of tiny yellow flowers all over it, and a white shawl around her shoulders.

'Here, I have something for you.' Charlotte took a glittering tiara from her small gathered bag.

Sally gasped. 'Is it appropriate?'

'Everyone has agreed. Alice and Kathryn. We want you to keep this. Alice was grateful for the other jewels, they paid for the deposit on the coach house and set John up in business. Those two are clearly besotted with each other. As soon as the steam train arrives in Cromer everyone will want a carriage to take them to their destinations. The business will thrive. I even caught Alice mucking out a stable the other day,' Charlotte laughed. 'It's so good to have her for a sister though we still have much to learn about each other. And Will, although as besotted as ever calls her 'Aunty Alice'. Thank you, for agreeing to let Kathryn come today. She has made up with Alice and come to the conclusion she has a headstrong daughter – or daughters should I say. Her husband will never accept me but I don't care. My home is here in this town. Kathryn is someone else in my life now. I imagine she will flit in and out, because of Alice mainly, she'll keep me hidden from her husband. And she will never replace you.'

'But she came today. It proves something,' said Sally, graciously.

Charlotte's meeting with Kathryn had been surreal. Kathryn came bearing gifts – matching outfits for her and Alice – *Sunday best for my daughters!* she'd said. And other gifts yet to be opened.

Kathryn wasn't like her portrait anymore, she had grey hair and a lined face, and she was shorter than Charlotte had imagined and she had grown portly. But there was no mistaking the resemblance between them. Kathryn had taken Charlotte's hand with a firm, warm grip and told her she was sorry for letting her go. Charlotte believed her. She'd heard Alice talk about Kathryn's sleepless nights and endless crying for her. But she would never tell Sally that. For all appearances Kathryn kept her distance but there was much unsaid between them, there would be many conversations to come, but today was about her mother, Sally.

'Imagine, Mother. You shouldn't have to worry about money ever again after Henry found father's lost sovereigns.'

'Yes. Imagine that. All those years I thought the reward had been lost and it was there all the time right under the floorboards under my bed.'

'And now you have it, Henry shouldn't have to do his foreign trading so much,' Charlotte laughed and added, 'The bells are ringing.'

279

'Aye, for calm waters.'

'You are so much better, mother. I never thought I'd see the day.'

Sally patted her hand. 'I'm so sorry for what I put you through for so long. And for all the secrets.'

'I know. And we both know it wasn't your fault. It was circumstances and laudanum, mostly laudanum.'

They walked together down the tree lined path towards town, the blue sea in the distance awash with billowing sails of tall ships and schooners.

Inside the church, the pews were full. Charlotte's class of children all stood, how they thrived under her teachings, how easy the change had been when the old school mistress left and they'd asked her to temporarily step in. She glanced at her father's loyal old friends, fishermen, lifeboat men, townsfolk and their wives. There was Kathryn and her son James, and Alice and John. And Will, so smart, at the front of the church standing next to a dapper looking Henry.

She walked halfway down the aisle with her mother and watched her walk slowly towards Henry. Beside her was a shuffle. She had tears streaming down her face, she wiped them with the back of her hand.

'Shall we, Miss Mayhew-Merryweather?'

'Aye, Captain O'Rourke. I think we might.'

And together with a rustle of her beautiful blue dress she thought she'd never see again, they passed the crew of the 'Merganser' including young Peter wearing Will's tweed cap and the too-small jacket, and also Mrs Johnson (but not Aunt Mary who had been told to stay behind at Summerville House. Nicholas would kindly let her carry on living there as before, for at least as long as Nicholas still traded at the docks).

Charlotte could hear herring gulls crying on the roof outside, and she thought they might soar and sweep over their new house on the cliffs overlooking the sea, where she had ten bedrooms. Imagine that, all those rooms and what she could with them. And those tall windows where she would watch for sails on the horizon.

And she stood at the front of the church next to her mother and Henry, waiting for her turn to make the sacred vow to her captain.

Acknowledgements:

I would like to thank the following tutors from my time at The University of East Anglia: Helen Ivory, Ashley Stokes, Sarah Law and Anna Reckin. Special thanks to Amanda Griffiths.

I would like to thank Cromer Lifeboat museum for informative displays and lifeboat models.

Also Cromer museum, which houses an old working laundry outbuilding amongst other historical information and objects into the working lives of fishermen and families back in the day.

Bibliography:

Cromer Preservation Society Guides 2, 6 and 8.

http://www.norfolkdialect.com/glossary

http://www.parishregistar.com/londons_docks.asp

About the author:

Lynn fell in love with Cromer Town whilst on holiday and moved there in the seventies. Her work has ranged from sewing buttons on cardigans to working as a lab technician in an all-girls school. Eventually she gained a BSc (Hons) with The Open University and settled to teach Field Studies at outdoor centres in Norfolk.

Alongside work she studied with Adult Education at the University of East Anglia and gained three Diplomas in Creative Writing (fiction and poetry) and a Post Graduate Certificate in poetry (with distinctions). She has appeared in numerous magazines, anthologies and competitions for poetry. Lynn has two poetry collections published with Indigo Dreams Publishing and writes reviews for Reach Poetry magazine under her married name. This is her first published full length novel.

Find out more about the author online at:

www.lynnwoollacott.co.uk

Printed in Poland
by Amazon Fulfillment
Poland Sp. z o.o., Wrocław